MW01145983

Broken
Lantern

Tina Arnold

Copyright © 2019 Tina Arnold

All rights reserved.

ISBN:
9781693157578

DEDICATION

To everyone that bought and supported Sweet Lantern,
and to those that pushed for this second book to be
written; thank you for believing in this story and in me.
You kept me going

Book Cover by

DarkWorksX @ Pixabay.com

This is a work of fiction. Names, characters, businesses, places, events, and incidents are either the products of the author's imagination or used in a fictitious manner. Any resemblance to actual persons, living or dead, or actual events is purely coincidental.

CHAPTER ONE

The days following Darry's death were nothing more than a blur. I didn't even want to be alive, much less eat or drink anything like our moms kept trying to push on me. I knew that I needed to take care of myself for the baby, but I just couldn't. I couldn't even bring myself to lay in our bed; I slept on the couch instead.

Everything just feels... off. I feel like my emotions are very raw and all over the place. I've lashed out at my family and Darry's too, more than once, not really meaning to but just unable to control myself. I've been avoiding everyone because of this. I don't want to hurt anyone's feelings but I'm having such a difficult time trying to hold my world together right now.

The guys that hit the back of Matt's Jeep all went to jail because of the chase that they had started through town. There were too many witnesses for them to walk away.

My world had changed so dramatically in the blink of an eye, and I was having a difficult time adjusting, to say the least. Darry was there every day, even before he was my husband, he was my best friend in this whole godforsaken world. He made everything better, lighter somehow; he made me better. And now he's gone, and I'm all alone. And here very soon, I'll have a baby to take care of, also alone. I have no idea how I'm going to get myself to function properly again, much less be able to care for a needy baby.

When it was me and Darry, I was excited for this new life of ours, but now I'm just scared, and I can't understand for the life of me why God would do this to us? *Why God? Why would you allow this to happen?* I'm just so sad, and so angry; at God, at the whole world. It's not fair.

I've been so out of it that I haven't a clue as to what day it is, or even whether it's night or day, when I wake up. I've covered every window with blankets and closed every door from all of the rooms off the livingroom. I don't want to see the sun at all.

When I'm awake, every time I close my eyes, my mind flashes back to seeing Darry's broken and bloody body lying on that hospital bed and then I get random flashes of his funeral and memorial service. I had had him cremated, because that's how he had always said he wanted to be taken care of.

I couldn't even get myself dressed for his funeral. My mom had to come over and put me into a black dress, even putting my shoes on my feet. My daddy helped me out to his truck, lifting me up into the passenger seat and buckling me in.

All I keep hearing are Darry's last words to me; "...tell my son I love him." It's not fair! Darry will never get to see on our child. He won't be there to hold my hand and support me during the birth of our baby either. The baby will never know how wonderful his father was and how much he loved him. He won't grow up with a daddy to throw the ball around with or to teach him to ride a bike. He won't have Darry here to ask for advice or to teach him how to tie a tie for his first school dance.

Darry was robbed too. He was too young to be taken like this. His life had just started. Our life together, as husband and wife, had just started.

I feel the anger building in me again, so I pick up a pillow and throw it across the room as hard as I can.

"Huh?! What was that?" I hear a voice coming from the dark corner where I threw the pillow. "Alice?"

I panic and turn on the lamp beside me. "Kevin? What are you doing here?"

He's sitting in the recliner in the corner, and by the looks of him, he's been there all night. His clothes are disheveled and his hair's a mess. He's got a small throw blanket over him and there's a couch pillow beside his feet on the floor, next to the one I just threw at him.

"We didn't want you to be alone. I volunteered to stay so your dad could go home and get some rest", He tells me, blushing. "But I've been here, even when someone else is here. I just want to make sure you're ok."

"My dad? He's been here too?" I ask, not fully understanding that they've obviously had a rotation going for babysitting me.

"Yeah, we've all been taking turns sitting with you, Alley."

"Kevin?"

"Yeah?"

"Please don't call me that."

"Oh, yeah... yeah... I'm sorry, I won't", he says, looking down at the floor.

"I don't mean to be rude, Kevin... that's what Darry calls..." I sigh, and start again, "...called me." I tell him, feeling ashamed of myself for making him feel uncomfortable.

"Oh no, I understand, no explanation needed, really", he says, his voice full of sincerity. "Can I get you something to eat or drink?" I can see the concern in his face.

"A glass of water would be nice", I tell him, and he smiles, getting up to retrieve a glass for me.

He comes back into the room and hands me a glass of ice water.

"Thank you, Kevin."

He nods and sits back down in the recliner. Waiting for me to speak to him, I assume.

"What day is it?" I ask, wanting to know how long I've been out of it.

"It's Saturday, Alle..er, Alice", he says and looks at his feet again. "It's been over two weeks. You had all of us scared. They'll all be so happy to know that you're ok."

"I'm not ok, Kevin. I don't think I'll ever be ok again", I say more to myself really. He nods his head in

4

understanding and sits back, letting his head fall back against the recliner, he stares at the ceiling, concentrating like he's in deep thought.

"I can't say I know exactly how you feel, but I do understand your pain, Alice. I loved him too. He was my best friend. I don't think I'll ever understand why God took him but let the rest of us live. He had so much more to live for." The pain in his voice catches me off guard. I look at him again and it's like I'm seeing him for the first time.

His face has several cuts on it. He's got a gash under his right eye that seems to be healing up well. He's got a cut down his left cheek, also starting to heal. There are bruises on him too, on his forehead and his arms. The sight of him now shocks me and I gasp.

"What's wrong?" he asks. "I just hadn't realized that you were hurt", I answer looking down at my legs stretched out in front of me on the couch, ashamed that I hadn't noticed his injuries sooner.

"Oh, no. I'm ok, really. It looks bad, but I'm alright. Matt and Joel got it a lot worse. Joel's still in the hospital", he tells me, worry in his expression.

"And Matt?" I ask.

"Oh, he's at home now, but he had us worried for a few days. He's got whiplash, and a few bad cuts and bruises. He had a concussion, but he's ok now, as far as that goes anyway. Joel's the one we're worried about. He's in a coma. He and Darry were both thrown from the car, neither of them were wearing a seat belt."

I draw in a deep breath when he mentions Darry's name and the accident. The pain hitting me right in the chest.

"I'm so sorry, Alice. If I had realized they weren't wearing it, I would've told them..." he drops his head and covers his face with his hands as he sobs into them.

I'm across the livingroom before I know I've moved, wrapping my arms around him. I lay my head on his shoulder and he wraps his arms around me, as we both cry about our horrible loss.

CHAPTER TWO

When we can breathe again, Kevin speaks first, asking if I want him to fix me a sandwich or something. He wipes his nose with the back of his sleeve and grabs a piece of his t-shirt hem to wipe the tears from his face, exposing the little trail of dark hair just below his belly button.

"Alice, I know how badly you're hurting, but you have to feed that baby, and more than a few bites of a pb and j. She needs something real, and so do you."

His words hit me in the heart, and I nod, agreeing to eat something.

"Awesome!" he exclaims, clapping his hands together and standing up. "I'm going to see what's in the kitchen." He walks off, leaving me to sit on the couch, wiping my own tears from my cheeks. My face burns from the salt and I can already feel the puffiness in my eyes.

A few minutes go by and Kevin pokes his head around the corner, "Hey, there's actually not much in here. You want me to order a pizza instead?"

I nod and start to tell him what I like, but he interrupts me before I can get it out. "Pepperoni, bacon and pineapple with stuffed crust, right?"

I look at him and raise an eyebrow, unsure of how he knows my pizza toppings. He just grins, saying, "I've heard you say it before." He shrugs and turns around, going back to the kitchen to call in the order.

A few minutes later, he comes back in and sits next to me on the couch. He doesn't say anything at first, but just puts his arm around my shoulders, letting me rest my head on him. It feels nice to be held, but I wish it was Darry sitting here with me.

"What's wrong with Joel?" I ask, wanting to break up the silence around us, and really wanting to know how he's doing.

Kevin's hesitant to talk about it at first. He doesn't answer me right away, so I turn to look up at him. He looks down at me, and I see the sadness in his once bright, cheerful eyes. He breaks eye contact and looks away, looking down at his knees, unsure whether he should tell me or not. "It's ok, Kevin, really. I want to hear it... all", I tell him, assuring him that I won't freak out.

"Alice, they were both thrown from the Jeep as it was flipping over. Matt and I had our seat belts on, but they didn't. Joel was thrown into a tree, breaking three of his ribs and fracturing his skull; he has swelling and bleeding on his brain. They have him in a medically induced coma, so he'll be comfortable. They're hoping that the swelling and bleeding will get under control, but right now they don't know what to expect, there could be brain damage. They just don't know very much right now." He begins to blink rapidly and turns his head up to the ceiling, and I know he's fighting back the tears again.

"Go on..." I tell him, wanting to hear this, but not wanting to at the same time.

"Alice? Are you sure?" he asks, looking down into my eyes. I can see the tears in his now and it breaks my heart.

I nod him on, bracing myself, because I know this next part is going to hurt like crazy.

He pulls me closer to him and begins to tell me how my husband died.

"Darry was thrown into the street. There was a truck coming in the other lane. He was thrown from the Jeep as it was beginning to roll." He takes a deep breath and I can feel his body shaking under me. "He slammed the truck so fast; the driver didn't even have time to hit the brakes." His tears are falling now, I can feel them sinking into my hair.

"The impact broke his back and both of his legs. The grill of the truck cut into his abdomen, damaging his liver badly." He's barely able to get the words out, but he pushes on for me. "His left arm was shattered, and his right wrist was fractured. There were head injuries too. They tried everything they could, they really did, Alice, but they couldn't save him. It was just too bad."

I feel his chest rising and falling quickly, and the tears are falling silently down my cheeks.

"Did he suffer?" I ask, bracing myself to hear the answer.

"They don't know. The doctors told his parents that they don't think he was able to feel anything after his back was broken, but they can't really know that." He tells me, honestly, "Matt said he was next to Darry when they picked him up, and it wasn't good."

He brings his other arm around and wraps me fully in his embrace, letting me cry into his chest, his head bent down, his chin resting on the top of my head.

The doorbell rings and Kevin shifts, wiping his face with his shirt again. He walks over to the door and opens it. Greg Howser is standing at the door in his Perry's Pizzeria delivery uniform, a depressingly sad look on his face. He tries to smile a half smile at us and hands the box to Kevin, saying, "It's on the house, dude. Perry wouldn't even think about charging her. He said to tell her that if she needs anything else, just let him know." Kevin nods and thanks him, telling him to thank Perry for us.

He turns around and asks where I want to eat. I point to the coffee table and he comes into the livingroom, sitting the box down in front of me. He grabs a tissue from one of the many tissue boxes around us and hands it to me. "I'm going to refill your glass and get me a drink and I'll be right back, ok?" I nod and he turns to leave.

I sit staring at the box, tracing the letters repeatedly with my eyes, trying hard not to concentrate on the devastating details of my best friend's death.

I feel numb... empty, really, like my heart has been ripped from my chest and thrown far away from me, never to be seen again.

Kevin comes back with our waters and sits down next to me. Just as my daddy comes through the front door.

"Hey kiddo. How are you feeling? I saw Greg's truck pulling down the drive, so you're ready to eat, huh?" he says, as he comes to sit on the other side of me. He pulls me into him and kisses the top of my head. "I love you, baby girl." I can't even cry anymore. I'm just give out. I hug my daddy tighter and tell him, "I love you too, Daddy."

.

CHAPTER THREE

I missed my ultrasound because it was scheduled for the day after the accident. Kevin has been here with me all week, refusing to leave my side and trying to get me to go to the doctor for my missed appointments. He's pushed for me to reschedule the ultrasound, but I just don't feel like I'm ready to leave the house yet.

I know he can't be comfortable sleeping in that recliner or on the floor, which he has started sleeping on now, but he says he's perfectly fine. He said he doesn't want me to be alone, and that he is staying until I tell him he has to go. He's only left to go get a change of clothes and to take a shower once or twice when someone else was here with me.

It's very sweet and thoughtful of him, and I appreciate it very much, but I know he wants to go see Matt and to check on Joel. And he needs to go back to school too.

He's getting updates through text messages about Joel every day, but I know it's not the same.

He says Jess has been by Joel's side the whole time. She hasn't left the hospital once. Her dad had to bring clean clothes to her there because she refused to walk out of his room. She only leaves the room briefly when the nurses need privacy and even then, she just steps outside of the door and is right back again as soon as they call her in.

I know how she feels. And I hate that she's feeling it.

"Who's there for her though, Kevin?" I had asked him, not wanting her to be sitting there crying and hurting with no one to lean on.

"Their families are alternating staying with the two of them. His mom and dad, her mom and dad, and his sister have all stayed with her up there." he told me, reassuring me that she's got support.

I still don't feel like eating, but Kevin forces me to eat at least one good meal a day and he makes me take a few bites of a sandwich for breakfast or lunch.

"You have to eat, Alley" he said to me earlier this afternoon. I hit him in the arm. "Sorry, I mean, Alice."

"The baby has to have food", he reminded me, handing me a plate with half a pb an j and apple slices.

"I know, thank you", I told him, taking the plate and eating the apple slices. "I honestly don't know what I'd do without you."

He looked up, taken aback for a split second and then he smiled at me. "I wouldn't be anywhere else." He said to me, handing me a glass of milk.

He's been very patient with me. When I lose it and snap at him for hovering or for telling me to eat for the hundredth time, he doesn't get upset with me. Instead he hugs me and tells me it'll be ok. He'll put the plate of food on the table next to me and go outside to sit on the porch until I calm down. He amazes me, because I don't think I'd be as calm as he has been if someone was being that ugly to me.

After a long day of watching tv, talking and napping, it's dinner time. I eat the latest chicken casserole that Kevin's made and finish the glass of lemonade, sitting the empty dishes on the coffee table and lay my head back to look up at the ceiling. He's sitting beside me on the floor, his back up against the couch where I'm lying, his legs stretched out in front of him, his empty plate and glass next to him. He's watching the news with a very serious, very focused look on his face. And I begin to drift off to sleep to the sound of the weatherman telling us about next week's forecast.

I'm back in the hospital. The long corridor in front of me getting longer and longer as I try my hardest to run to the end of it. The lights are flickering all around me, I hear crying and screaming but there's no one there, it's completely empty. It looks like the apocalypse has passed through here, machines are overturned and scattered around the floors, hospital beds are turned over on their sides, blocking doorways. There's trash and other debris everywhere, and there's blood all over everything. I finally make it to the door that I'm looking for and turn to go into the room. There's a body on the bed before me, the room looks to be in the same condition as the rest of the hospital. I walk over to the bed and look down to see Darry's bloody face and broken body laid out before me. His eyes open suddenly, and he grabs my arm, but his face isn't his face anymore, it's Kevin's. I scream and scream, trying to break away from his hands...

"Alice!" Alice! Wake up!" I'm being shaken frantically. My eyes open and I sit straight up on the couch. I'm looking into Kevin's face; he looks distressed, his eyes puffy and his hair disheveled, like he was just sleeping too. I look down on the floor beside the couch and see his pillow and blanket there beside me. "Are you ok? You were screaming pretty loud. You scared the crap out of me." He says as he comes to sit beside me, trying to calm his frantic breathing.

"Oh, Kevin, it was awful" I cry, and he pulls me into his arms.

"It's ok, Alice. I'm here, you're safe."

And in this moment, I'm very happy that he's here. I'm suddenly so thankful that he hasn't allowed me to be alone. I don't think I could do this alone.

"Can you stay with me tonight, please?" I ask him, quietly.

"I wasn't going anywhere. I told you, I'm not leaving until you tell me to." He says, trying to assure me that he's not leaving my side anytime soon.

"I mean, here, on the couch. Will you lay with me and just hold me, please? While we sleep..." I say, embarrassed and unsure if he will be ok with it.

I see his cheeks flush and he nods, scooting up behind me. He wraps me in his arms and pulls me toward him, resting my back against his chest. I feel safe and comforted as I drift off to sleep again, praying that I don't return to that awful hospital.

CHAPTER FOUR

We're sitting in the waiting room, it's unbelievably cold and even in Kevin's Varsity jacket, I'm shivering. I don't want to be here. I know I need to be, but this feels wrong somehow. It's not supposed to be Kevin sitting next to me right now, though I am very grateful to him for bringing me and for staying here with me.

Honestly, if it wasn't for him making this appointment and telling me he'd carry me all the way here if he had to, I wouldn't even be here in the first place.

Kevin had insisted that I see my doctor, even if I didn't want the ultrasound, although he had gone ahead and scheduled that too, "just in case", he had told me.

I lay my head on his shoulder and he wraps his arm around me, running his hand up and down my arm, trying to warm me up. "Do you want me to ask them to turn the heat up?"

"No, they keep it cold to keep the germs away", I tell him, not knowing if it's true or not but knowing that I'd heard it somewhere before. "And they wouldn't turn it up for just one person anyway but thank you."

"I'll find the thermostat and turn it up myself." He says, starting to stand up. He sounds oddly protective and very sure of himself. I just smile at him and shake my head, pulling him back down into the chair and leaning into him more. He holds me tighter and starts scrolling through his phone.

"Matt wants to know if he can stop by tonight with Britt?" he tells me, asking if I'm up for a visit. I nod my head and tell him I think that it would be nice to see them. He smiles and texts Matt back telling him it'll be fine; we'll be home around 5pm.

"Home, huh?" I say to him, raising an eyebrow and grinning.

"I didn't mean *my* home", he says, blushing.

"I'm just messing with you, Kevin. I think you do kind of live there right now though." I laugh and he grins at me, shrugging his shoulders. "I guess I kinda do." He laughs and adds, "I told you I'd go when you wanted me to."

"I like having you there. I don't want to be alone." I tell him as the door opens and they call me back. We walk down a hall and turn into the first room we come to. I silently thank God that the doctor's office doesn't look anything like the hospital. I don't think I would have been able to walk in here today had it resembled those corridors in any way. Just the thought of it makes me sick to my stomach.

"You ok?" Kevin breaks me away from my thoughts. "You're turning kind of pale there." He says, pulling the little black trashcan up in front of me.

"I'm ok. Just thinking about... stuff."

The doctor comes in and I'm so happy that I chose a female gynecologist. "How are we feeling today, Mrs. Williams?" she asks, making my heart hurt. "Can you call me Alice, please." I ask, looking over at Kev and then down at the floor, ashamed at not wanting to hear my married name.

"Yes, of course, Alice it is. So how are you feeling today, Alice? Has the baby been moving a lot? Are you feeling sick at all?" She asks, obviously taking note of my pallid complexion.

"I'm ok, I was just thinking of Darry..." my voice trails off and she nods as though she understands what I was going to say. She doesn't linger on it, which is nice, and I am grateful when she moves on to giving me a once over, making sure everything is ok with growth and such.

"Are you eating, Alice?" she asks, and turns to look at Kevin who nods at her, telling her that he's making sure I eat.

"Ok, because you have to eat, you know that, right? We can't stop eating, even if we don't feel like it." She says to me, with a very serious expression on her face. I nod and promise to eat more.

"Good girl", she says, patting my knee and grabbing my hand to bring me down to the floor in front of the exam table. She hands me a cup and tells me to fill it halfway and sends me down the hall to the restroom.

I know the drill by now and do as I'm told.

When I make it back to the room, the ultrasound tech is waiting for me, ready to take me back for the gender reveal. My stomach moves under the gown and I bring my hand to my belly.

"The baby is getting ready to show off for us", the tech says, smiling at me. She turns to Kevin and tells him we'll be right back. He smiles and says ok, he'll be right here.

"What? No. No way. I wouldn't have even come to this if it wasn't for him. He's coming back with me." I tell her, with a sharp tone and grab Kevin's hand pulling him to his feet. "Let's go", I say.

The tech agrees and starts out of the room, Kev smiling as I pull him with me.

"Yes, ma'am", he says, and follows me, not letting go of my hand. I turn to see him grinning and shaking his head, laughing at my bossiness.

I can't help but smile back at him. He's letting me pull him through the hallway of this doctor's office, while he's just a-smiling.

When we get in the room, it's very dark except for the lights of the monitor and a very dim yellow light over the head of the bed. The tech instructs me to get on the table and lay down. She asks if it's ok to pull the gown up, exposing my underwear in front of Kevin. I hadn't thought of that when I had insisted that he come with us. It just didn't cross my mind.

I look at Kevin who is fully red faced now and looking like he's going to turn and run out of the door any minute now.

"Yes, it's fine", I tell her, grabbing Kevin's hand and squeezing it. "Are you ok to stay with me, though?" I ask, praying he says yes.

"Of course. I won't leave until you tell me to, remember." He says and smiles, sitting in the chair next to the bed, keeping my hand in his the whole time.

The tech raises my gown and begins to put a very cold gel on my belly. Kevin keeps his eyes on my face or the monitor the whole time, trying very hard to be a gentleman. She stops before putting the probe on me and asks, "Do you want to know the sex of the baby, Alice?" I shake my head and Kevin looks at me with a surprised look on his face. "Alice are you sure?" he asks. "Yeah, will you tell him though, away from me, please?" I ask the nurse, still looking into Kevin's eyes. She agrees as me and Kev exchange a small smile.

I look at the monitor briefly just to see the baby's heart beating and I'm in awe of the shape of mine and Darry's child there on the screen in front of us. It's a black and white image, and I can make out the shape of the head, the side of the face; nose and all. The tiny little arm, hand and fingers are at the mouth, like the baby is sucking its thumb. I feel the tears coming, so I turn away from the monitor and watch Kevin's expressions as he watches everything the tech is doing and showing him. He is very focused, and his eyes are lit up as they shift from here to there, taking it all in. He looks at me and smiles, squeezing my hand gently.

"You ok?" he whispers.

"Yeah, I'm good."

The tech finishes up taking pictures and wipes the gel from my belly. She tells me to hold tight while she takes Kevin out into the hall to tell him the sex of the baby. I sit up and let my feet dangle from the edge of the tall table, waiting as patiently as possible.

When they come back into the room, Kevin smiles at me through tears. He's holding sonogram photos, that he shoves into his back pocket. He doesn't say a word, he just walks over to me and hugs me, lifting me from the bed into his arms. He rests his chin on my shoulder and asks, "Are you sure you don't want to know?" I tell him, "No, I don't want anyone else to know either." He pulls back, sitting me down on the bed, grabbing my shoulders, he looks at me, his brow furrowed. "What? Alice... no. I can't do that. Your parents... his parents, they all want to know. I don't even have a right to know."

"Kevin, I don't want anyone else to know, please, for me?"

He pulls me into his arms again and agrees not to say anything to anyone. "Can we go home now?" I ask and he helps me down off the table so I can go get my clothes back on.

CHAPTER FIVE

When we pull into the driveway, I see my mom and Elaine standing on the front porch of my parents' house. They walk down the steps and wait at the last one for Kevin to pull in and park. He comes around to open my door for me, taking my hand to help me up. "How do I tell them that I know but you don't want me to tell anyone?" he asks, and I can hear the shakiness in his voice. He's a good man, he loves Darry's family and he's really come to love mine too. I know he doesn't want to keep this from them, but for some reason, I just can't bring myself to know. I know for sure, if our parents know, someone will let it slip and I really don't want to know.

I turn to our moms standing there on the bottom step, smiling excitedly, waiting to hear whether they're having a grandson, or a granddaughter and I say to them, "I don't know the sex of the baby. I don't want to know. I know you both are anxious to know, and you were looking forward to me pulling in and telling you, but I just couldn't do it." They stop smiling and look from me to Kevin and back to me again in disbelief. "What? Why? Did you not have the ultrasound then?" My mom asks, her voice trembling. Elaine hears it too and wraps her arm around my mom's shoulder, hugging her.

"I did. The baby is healthy and growing as it should." I tell them, trying to give them some good news.

Elaine speaks up, "You had the ultrasound, but they didn't tell you the sex?" She looks at both of us suspiciously.

"I know the sex", Kevin speaks up for me. "I'm so sorry", he says, putting his head down and turning to walk back to my house, shaking his head and kicking rocks in frustration all the way.

"What?!" My mom yells. "He knows? You let Kevin know, but we, the grandparents, we can't know? How is that even fair, Alley?"

Elaine looks at me, tears in her eyes, but she's much calmer than my mom. "Alice, dear, can you please tell us why you chose to let Kevin know but you don't want us to know?" My heart breaks for her and my mom, but I can't risk them letting it out.

"I don't want to know", I say, fighting back tears, hearing my voice begin to shake. "I don't want to hurt anyone's feelings, and I don't want y'all to feel any more pain, but I can't risk it getting out and getting back to me. Please understand. I know that Kevin will never utter a word, to anyone. But you two and daddy and Bobby, y'all are so excited, as you should be, and I know it could slip out on accident and it would spread like wildfire through this small town. It would be back to me before dinner."

Elaine nods her head, understanding completely and comes over to hug me. "I get it, Alice. I really do. I respect your decision. I'm just happy to hear that you and the baby are healthy."

My mom is not happy, but she agrees with Elaine and hugs me before she turns to walk into her house, without saying a word.

I walk back to my house and walk inside, not really knowing what to expect. I know he's not happy. And I've never really seen Kevin upset before.

"I didn't like doing that, Alley. It's not fair to them. I shouldn't know this and them not know!" He says, pacing the length of the livingroom, his hands flying around as he speaks.

"I get it, Kev. I understand the frustration. But can you please try to understand where I'm coming from?" I beg him, sitting on the couch. "Darry was so sure that we were having a boy..." I begin to cry and bring my hands up to cover my face. Kevin is across the room in a second, falling to his knees in front of me, pulling me into his arms. I feel his lips push against my hair, but he doesn't dare kiss me. "Alley, please don't cry. I won't tell anyone. You know I won't."

I don't even care that he has called me Alley twice now. It's starting to feel normal to hear it again. Soothing even. He says it just the way Darry did. So soft and sweet and gentle, and full of... love? No. I'm just missing Darry, I tell myself and shake off the silly thought.

"It's going to be hard not to tell you though. I hope I don't slip up." He tells me, worried that he will let it out. "And how the heck am I not going to start buying baby stuff now, knowing what we should be buying?"

I pull back and look at him, questioning his choice of words.

"You know what I mean." He says, "Don't be a dork."

I laugh and he laughs too, and the room seems to lighten up around us.

"What time will they be here?" I ask, wanting to be sure to have the house and myself somewhat presentable when they get here.

"I told them 5pm, I hope that's ok."

I look through the door to see the clock on the microwave in the kitchen. It's 3:32 now, so I need to get up and start moving.
"I don't want them to walk into the house with it like this", I tell him, looking around at all the blankets on the windows. The house itself is really clean, he's been keeping it up for me, so I didn't have to worry about it. I seriously don't know what it would look like if he hadn't stayed with me. I can't even tell you how many times he's cleaned my vomit or picked up broken shards of glass from me throwing something against the wall just to hear something break because I was so angry. Not angry at him, just at the world, at my situation, at losing my best friend and husband. But he hasn't said a word. He's just been here, cleaning me up and helping me get through each day and night.

Nights are the worst. He has had to take to staying on the couch with me every night due to the nightmares. But he doesn't seem to mind. He holds me and when I wake up screaming, he brings me back and helps me settle down enough to get back to sleep. I'm so glad that he was Darry's best friend and that he loved him enough to take care of me now.

Kevin is up on his feet, starting to take the blankets down as soon as I mention it. As each blanket falls, the sun shines into the house more and more, which would be ok, except that with each new ray of light, another picture frame is lit up. Darry's beautiful face is looking at me from all directions. I feel my head begin to spin and before I can stop it, the contents of my stomach have risen in my throat and are spilling out all over the floor at my feet.

"Alice!" Kevin is at my side, grabbing my hair in his hands, pulling it into a ponytail behind me as I lean forward and continue to dry heave.

"Oh man, Alice. What in the... what happened? Are you ok?" he asks, walking me over to sit in the recliner, getting me as far from the mess as possible. I can't speak, I just point, all around us, to each picture of his smiling face. "Please... just take them... Kevin, get them away from me, please."

He looks sad, but he moves away from me, slowly taking each one down. He grabs our wedding photo and then he starts taking away Darry's baby pictures and photos of us through our years growing up together. He takes them and puts them all into the hall closet and comes back for the last one. The one on the wall over the back of the recliner that I'm sitting in now. It's a large photo of our little motley crew taken only a week before his death.

We're standing in front of the football field, Matt and Brittany, Joel and Jessica, me and my baby bump, and Darry and Kevin. He had jumped on Darry's back just as Coach had pushed the button to snap the photo, one arm around Darry's chest and the other in the air over his head, like he's riding a bull. Both boys were laughing like crazy. We were all so happy, smiling and loving life... loving each other. We were invincible. Nothing could touch us.

Kevin lingers on the image in his hands, tracing over it with his finger as he walks away and disappears into the hallway. He comes back with towels and cleaner for the vomit on the carpet.

"I'm so sorry, Kevin." I tell him, upset with myself for not having better control. "No", He says to me, bending down to clean the carpet. "You don't apologize to me, Alice. I can't even begin to understand what this is doing to you. I loved him too, but it's not the same. I don't mind this." He says, pointing to the mess in front of him.

I leave the recliner and walk over to him and he stands up, facing me, looking at me not understanding what I'm doing. I stand on my tiptoes and throw my arms around his neck. He wraps me in his arms and bends down to allow me to snuggle close to his neck. "Thank you, Kevin. Thank you so much for being here. Darry was lucky to have a friend like you, someone that loved him enough to be here for him even in death."

I feel his body go rigid in my arms and he pulls back, breaking my arms from around his neck and setting me down on my feet in front of him, leaving me confused. He bends down and starts cleaning again and I turn to sit down, not understanding why he reacted that way.

He comes back into the room with me, bringing me a glass of water. "Here, drink this. It'll help you feel better and settle your stomach. You should probably take a shower really quick and I'll finish taking down the blankets and getting rid of things you don't want to see. Ok?"

I nod and drink the water, before sitting the glass down beside me and taking off to go to the guest bathroom. When I get to the door, I turn on the light and see Kevin's stuff set neatly around the sink. His razor, deodorant, his Axe body spray that I love so much, and his toothbrush and toothpaste. When I pull back the shower curtain, I see his shampoo and conditioner sitting on the side of the tub. The whole bathroom smells like him now from all of the showers he's taken in here recently. I take in a deep breath, smelling the now familiar scent and go to brush my teeth. When I'm done, I drop my clothes to the floor, and step into the shower. I let the hot water cascade down my body, lifting me up and taking me far away from here.

I allow my thoughts to drift, to the ocean and the aquarium, driving down the coast in a cherry red convertible, feeling the wind in my hair and hearing the water hits the rocks below the cliffs. I hear his voice, his laughter in my mind. I feel the calming come over me and then I see his bloody face and feel his hand grasping mine as he tells me he loves me more than anything and then I watch again as he slips away, leaving me all alone. I scream, sliding down the shower wall to the floor. The bathroom door flies open, and Kevin pulls the curtain back, exposing my naked crumpled up body to him.

"What is it?! Alley! Are you ok?" His eyes are wild, his chest is rising and falling fast. The terrified look in his eyes is all I remember before everything starts to go black and I feel his arms swoop in around me, lifting me up and out of the tub.

CHAPTER SIX

I wake up to muffled voices coming from the livingroom. I look down to see that I'm dressed in my nightgown, but I don't remember putting it on.

"She's hanging in there, man, but it's been touch and go, for real." Kevin's in the livingroom, talking to someone. My head feels heavy and I can't see anything. The room around me feels strange; I don't know where I am.

"Where are all of their photos?" I hear a girl ask.

"Don't mention them when she wakes up, please", Kevin begs the girl. She must have agreed because he says, "Thank you."

"Darry would be very happy with you, staying here like this, taking care of her and the baby." I hear a different male voice and then it hits me, Matt and Brittany are here.

I sit up and feel with my hands what I was laying on and turn to reach for a lamp. I flip the switch and begin to sob uncontrollably. I'm lying on our bed, covered with the very blanket that we used to make love under. Darry's pillow beside me, I reach over to pick it up and bring it to my nose. I take in his scent and the tears continue to fall.

Kevin comes in, turning on the overhead light; Matt and Brittany right behind him. Kevin comes over and kneels in front of me, putting his hands on my knees. He looks up into my eyes and I peak at him over the pillow that is clutched firmly to my chest. "I don't want to be in here, Kevin. Please." I whisper.

Without a word, he nods and stands up, swooping me up into his arms, he walks me out of the bedroom and takes me into the livingroom, sitting me down on the couch and then sitting next to me. I ball up, holding the pillow and turn toward Kevin. He wraps his arms around me and looks at Matt and Brittany who are just standing there, watching us in silence, a look of sympathy on both of their faces. Matt turns off the bedroom light and closes the door behind him. He walks over and sits down on the recliner, and Britt joins him, sitting on the arm of the chair.

"You ok?" She says, barely louder than a whisper, tears welling up in her eyes. I look at her and shake my head, "No", is all I can say. She nods, understanding and Matt gets up to cross the room. He bends down and kisses the top of my head, "Me either." He says, sitting next to me, turning me away from Kev and bringing me to him, he wraps his arms around me and we both cry. We're all four crying together in mine and Darry's livingroom, feeling every bit of the pain of our loss. The only sound is our sobs, echoing in my ears.

I hear the door open and close and look up to see the other Mrs. Williams walking across my floor straight to me. She kneels down in front of me, and says, "What can I do, Alice? Please tell me." Everyone is looking at me now, wiping the tears from their eyes. Silent tears are streaming down this beautiful face staring into mine. And I see Darry's eyes staring back at me. I feel instant calm wash over me. My sobs begin to slow. Elaine reaches over to the table beside us and brings back a tissue for me to blow my nose.

"Your being here is good." I tell her, smiling a weak smile at her.

"Let me cook for you kids, Alice." She says, getting up to go into the kitchen, but I stop her. "Thank you, Elaine, but I think... could you... can we get Chinese food?" I ask, and everyone looks at me, and then they all bust out laughing. "Yes, baby girl, we can get Chinese", she says, smiling.

"You can have anything you want", Kevin says to me, as he leaves the room to call the order in.

Elaine sits next to me, eating her sesame chicken and noodles, we're all sitting in the livingroom, circled around the coffee table; me, Kevin and Elaine on the couch and Matt and Brittany sitting with their legs criss-crossed on the floor in front of the table. We're all stuffing our faces as we share happy stories of Darry and our time spent with him. We aren't crying anymore, instead the house is full of laughter. My stomach hurts from laughing so much and my face is sore from smiling.

"There was this one time, we went into Henry's because Darry was buying a few crates of strawberries for you...." Kevin begins to tell us, "...he had just had tacos and was feeling really gassy. But he didn't want to wait until he was at the register to let it out and have to face old Ms. Holly when he let it rip. So, he backed up to the meat section and let it go. A lady came right over, not knowing what he was doing and started picking up packs of meat and sniffing them to see if they were good or not. Her face twisted and she got this look. I thought I was gonna bust trying not to laugh. She looked at Darry and held one up to him and said, "Smell this. All of this meat is rancid! They're all bad!" she told us, pointing to the entire lot of meat. We couldn't hold it in any longer and we both busted out laughing at her, walking away to go pay for your berries."

We're all rolling in laughter at the thought of this woman and the look on her face as she smelled Darry's fart all over the meat.

It feels so good to laugh again. And to see all of these people that I love, laughing as we all remember the silliness of someone that meant the world to each of us. Someone that at one time or another had lit up our world for one reason or another. Darry was so loved and so missed. He had touched the hearts of all of us and of so many others. It warms my heart to know that he will live on through all of us and the memories we each have of him and the memories we all share of him too.

I look at Kevin as he's laughing, and I feel a pull at my heart. I'm so glad he's able to let go for a while and laugh and enjoy himself. He's had it hard these past couple of weeks, taking care of me and dealing with me in my very worst moments. I am so grateful for him and his love for Darry. I'm so thankful that he loved him enough to be here for me.

He looks over at me and our eyes lock, his laughing slows to a smile and he winks at me. I smile and turn toward Matt and Brittany. Matt is telling about their locker room shenanigans and Britt is laughing at the thought of Darry putting icy hot into the jock strap of Kenny Thomas, the biggest jerk on the football team, because he said I was hot, and he was going to ask me out.

That's my Darry though... always looking out for me.

I finish the last bite of my honey chicken and slurp up the last of my noodles and reach over Kevin for my glass of water at the same time he's leaning up to grab his from the coffee table. We bump into each other and I turn to look at him at the wrong time, our lips brush and I pull back, turning to sit back against the couch quickly, looking away from him. My eyes go wide and my cheeks flush in embarrassment. The whole room is silent until Brittany and Elaine start laughing at us. I turn to look at Kevin and he's sitting back, looking at me, a grin across his face but his cheeks are just as red as mine feel. "You don't have to kiss me; you can just ask for your glass and I'll hand it to you." He says, teasing me. I slap his chest and he lets out an "Oof" sound, pulling his hand to his chest and bending over to act like I just punched him in the stomach.

The room is full of our belly laughs. The baby starts kicking like crazy and without realizing it, I grab Kevin's hand to put it on my belly. He stops laughing instantly, and just takes it in. The baby kicks against him and his eyes soften. He looks up at me, and I see the light in his eyes as he smiles at me. Then, before I know it, I have three other hands on me, as we all feel what can only be explained as the baby dancing in my belly.

"Man, she's going nuts in there!" Kevin says, excitedly and every hand falls away from me instantly.

I just look at him and shake my head. Elaine gasps and brings her hand to her mouth. Matt and Brittany are looking from Kev back to me, a look of surprise on their faces, and I know they're waiting for me to hit him again.

"She, huh?" I say, pressing my lips together.

"Oh my God, Alice. I'm so sorry. I'm soooo sooooo sorry!" Kevin pleads, begging me to forgive him. "I told you, I'd let it slip", he says, shaking his head, disappointed in himself.

"It's ok, Kevin. I'm ok, really." I tell him, running my hand up and down his arm.

"I have a granddaughter!!" Elaine says, jumping up from the couch and clapping her hands, now that she knows it's safe to do so.

"Can we please tell your parents now?" Kevin asks me, his voice full of both hope and relief.

I laugh and as soon as I nod, he runs out the front door before I can suggest that we call them.

CHAPTER SEVEN

When Kevin returns, he has both of my parents trailing behind him. My mom steps through the door with a huge "happy Grandma" smile plastered to her face. Daddy comes over and hugs me, telling me how happy he is for me. Mom and Elaine immediately start talking about pink dresses and ballet classes.

Kevin is standing beside my dad, a big grin on his face. He sees me looking and gives me a double thumbs up, and I can literally see the relief in his expression. He's ecstatic over being free of his burden of keeping such a big, unfair secret.

Brittany and Matt are talking about a baby shower when Britt suddenly stops and turns to me to ask, "What's her name?"

I look down and then back up at Kevin and smile. I turn to look at Brittany and Matt, telling her, "Dallas. Her name is Dallas." She smiles at me and nods, understanding why. "That's beautiful, Alice. I'm glad you decided to keep it for a girl too. Darry would have loved it."

Mom and Elaine excuse themselves after many hugs and kisses on the cheek. "We have so much to talk about, we're gonna go over to our house and talk over a hot cup of tea." Mom tells me as they're leaving.

Daddy kisses my forehead, whispering in my ear,

"Another baby girl to spoil", and he follows them out the door.

Matt and Brittany stand up to take their food trash into the kitchen and tell us they're heading over to the hospital to see if they can do anything to help Jessica and they want to tell her about the baby if it's ok with me. Of course, I'm fine with them telling her. She shouldn't be the only one to not know now. And she could probably use some good news, something to lighten the mood a little.

When everyone is gone, and it's just Kevin and me, we sit down and turn the tv on, as usual for our evenings lately. But tonight, he doesn't sit across the couch from me, he scoots up close and puts his arm around me, pulling me into him. I pull my legs in and lean toward him, dropping my head on his shoulder. "I'm really sorry for letting it out like that, Alice. I honestly didn't mean to." He tells me and I can hear the regret in his voice.

"It's ok, really. I'm kind of glad I know actually", I reassure him. "And honestly, it doesn't hurt like I thought it would."

"Good, I'm so relieved to hear you say that because I feel like a heavy weight has been lifted off my chest. I hated knowing when your parents didn't even know."

We sit watching some comedy show that Kevin stopped on for a few minutes and I ask, "I wonder if Darry knows it's a girl?"

"Darry knows everything now, Alley. He's watching over you two, you can bet on it. He wouldn't let anyone stop him from getting to you, even in death." He says, and I know he believes it.

I snuggle up to him more and he leans in to smell my hair, trying to be smooth about it but I hear him.

I pull back and look at him, trying not to laugh. "Did you just smell my hair?" He looks horrified. "Um..." I can't help but laugh. And before I know what's happening, Kevin pulls me into him and kisses me, parting my lips with his, he moves his tongue around mine and his hands go to the back of my head, as he kisses me deeper.

It feels so nice. I let myself melt into him, kissing him back, and Darry's face flashes into my mind.

I pull away and jump up off the couch. Moving to the recliner, I sit down and put my face in my hands.

"Oh, God! Alice, I'm so sorry. Alley, please..." He's in front of me, kneeling down, both hands on my knees. "Alice, please, I'm so sorry. Say something, please."

"I think you need to go, Kev. I'm sorry. Please don't be angry." I tell him, barely loud enough for him to hear me, but he does. He stands up straight. He nods, understanding and turns to leave the house. But before he walks out the door, he turns to me, and I look up at him. His eyes are watery, his face is red and he's shaking a bit. "I'm really sorry, Alley. I would never hurt you on purpose."

I smile a half smile and say, "Please don't call me that, Kevin." And he turns to walk out the door, closing it gently behind him, with all the weight of the world on his shoulders.

When he's gone, I lose it. I cry like a baby, my entire body shakes, hurting my ribs. I feel the baby start to move and know I have to calm down... for her. For my daughter.

I concentrate on her and soon my sobs subside into heavy breaths and then into nothing. I move over to the couch and lay down, pulling Darry's pillow up beside me. I pull my gown up and rub my belly while talking to her.

"Hi, baby girl", I start. "I'm sorry if I scared you crying like that. Mommy's just very sad right now. And confused too. Your daddy was the love of my life. He was my very best friend from day one. I've never lived without him before, and I'm not sure I'm doing a good job of it now, to tell you the truth. The voice you've been hearing, that's not your daddy, but you probably already know that, huh? Your daddy loved to talk to you. I'm sure you knew his voice from any other."

I stop to wipe my nose with a tissue and take a drink of water. I think I hear something move outside the livingroom window, but after waiting a few minutes I don't hear it anymore, so I start again.

"The voice you've been hearing is Kevin, one of your daddy's best friends. He's been wonderful to us since daddy... went to Heaven. He's been here for everything.

But I don't know what to feel about him. I love him for what he's done for us. I feel safe with him here. But I can't let someone else kiss me. I've only ever kissed your daddy. And he's not left much room in my heart for anyone else. It's too soon for me to feel anything for someone else... right?"

I look down and see her foot pushing at my belly. I smile and run my hand over it, as she kicks against me.

"I do love him though. But I don't know how right now. I can't even begin to think of loving someone like I love your daddy."

I fall asleep on the couch talking to my girl. My head's a jumbled-up mess of emotions and uncertainties, as I drift off to dream.

I wake up in a hospital gown, and it's covered in blood. The room around me smells rancid and the sound of beeping machines fills my ears, making it hard for me to think. The door is open, and a light is flickering just beyond it. I step out into the corridor and look around but all I see are dead bodies littering the floors and blood... blood is everywhere. I scream and turn around to see Kevin standing behind me, his eyes are white, like dead eyes. He reaches out for me, to grab me and I scream louder, turning to run from him.

"Alley!! Er... Alice! Alice!! Wake up. Please wake up." I hear Kevin's voice calling to me. I let my eyes flutter open and realize he's sitting on the edge of the couch, holding me in his arms.

"Wha... Kevin? What are you doing here? How did you know?" I ask him, confused and unable to understand what's happening.

"I never left, Alice. I was sleeping on the porch when I heard you crying and screaming. Oh God, that scream, Alice." I look at him and see the tears in his eyes. "Alice, I think you should talk to someone about these nightmares. The way you scream terrifies me, I know you can't be ok."

"What? What do you mean you never left?" I ask, pulling back to look at him. Trying to make sense of what he's just said to me. "You've... you mean, you've been out there the whole time?"

He looks down, ashamed or embarrassed or maybe a little of both. When he looks up again, I see the hurt in his eyes and the frown on his lips.

"Kevin, did you hear me earlier? Talking to Dallas, I mean?"

He nods his head and now I'm embarrassed. And maybe a bit ashamed of myself too.

"Kevin, I'm sorr..." I start to say, but he stops me. "Don't be, Alice. I understand. Really, I do. I must be stupid or something to think that you could love me, especially so soon, especially after loving Darry like you did."

He stops and puts his hands on either side of my face, lifting it to look at him. "Alice, I don't want to make you feel uncomfortable or make you feel obligated to me in any way. I just want to be here for you and Dallas. Please don't push me out. I don't expect you to love me like you loved him. I would never... but please let me stay and help you." He begs. "I do love you Alice, I've loved you since we were in the third grade, but there was no room for me, even then. No way I could have ever said anything. I know how he felt about you, because I felt it too, but you've always only had eyes for him, and I get that. I'm only telling you this now, so you know that I'm not here only for Daryl, Alley. I'm here because I want to be here... for you."

I can't say anything. I had no idea. Before that kiss, I honestly believed he was only here because I was carrying his best friend's baby and needed him to get through this. I would have never guessed he loved me. But now that I know, there's no going back from this. I love him too, even though it's not the same love I had for Darry. It's more of a deep love for a friend. A friend that has been here to see me through the darkest time of my life.

I can't speak. There are no words. I lay back and lift my blanket for him to crawl in beside me and he does, scooting up to me and pulling my back against his chest, we fall asleep in each other's arms, unsure of what tomorrow will bring for the both of us and our new situation.

CHAPTER EIGHT

The next day I wake up and turn to reach for Kevin, but he isn't there. I sit up, jumping up to my feet. I pray that he hasn't left because of what he heard last night. I can't take any more heart ache right now. I get dressed as quickly as possible, not even paying attention to the pangs in my chest as I crossed mine and Darry's bedroom to get to the closet.

Kevin has been going in to get my clothes for me and he takes them back and hangs them up or puts them away when they're washed again so that I don't have to go into that room. But he's not here now and I don't have time to think about anything else.

I run out of the house and see that his truck is still here next to Darry's car... well, my car. So where is he then? I called for him in the house, but he didn't answer. He wasn't in the kitchen either.

"Kevin?" I call out, hoping he will answer me.

Nothing.

"Keeeviiiiiin!" I call again, turning in every direction to see if he emerges.

Nothing.

I walk toward my parents' house thinking maybe he's there for some reason. When I turn the corner of their house, I hear laughter, but it's not coming from the house, it's a little distance away and muffled slightly. It's coming from... inside the barn?

I walk down and swing the big door open. Inside are Kevin, my dad and Mr. Williams. My dad and Mr. Williams are leaned over one of the stall doors, laughing their heads off at something inside. When they hear me open the door, they turn to look at me, still laughing, but trying hard to stop themselves.

Daddy lets go of the door and comes over to me, hugging me to him, he turns to walk me over to the stall, "Have yourself a good look there, baby girl. He's doing mighty fine, wouldn't ya say?" And he starts laughing again, as he pats me on the back and turns to walk into the office with Bobby following behind him.

Inside the stall is Kevin, and a beautiful white spotted mare, giving birth with his assistance. His face is green, and he keeps slipping in the wet hay, but he's steady trying. It's like watching an episode of an old comedy show. After a few minutes of me looking on in total awe of the miracle that's happening before my eyes, the foal is here and healthy. Everyone is fine, including Kevin, who looks nauseated and completely done in.

"Enjoy the show then, did you?" He asks, acting like he's going to throw the dirty gloves at me that he's taking off his hands.

He smiles at me and opens the door, "Sure did", I tell him, smiling at his busted ego.

He smiles back, "Well, let's go then", he says, grabbing my wrist and walking me over to the office.

He opens the door and tells Mom, Daddy and Mr. Williams that the foal is here and healthy and that he's turning in his card for the day because he's taking me to breakfast. They all agree and wave us on, smiling at us as Kevin closes the door.

"Well?" He asks, looking at me.

"Well, what?" I snap back. He grins and looks down, kicking the mud from his boots.

"Well, where do you want to go eat?" He asks, looking up at me slightly, cocking his head to the side.

I can't help but notice how handsome he looks. All sweaty and dirty; his blonde hair stuck to his forehead. The light from outside hitting his face just so, lighting up his already bright green eyes.

He's wearing a thin white t-shirt, and blue jeans, just like Darry used to wear. I think he's wearing Darry's old boots too. The sweat from his body has made the white shirt see through in some areas, showing off the skin underneath. I feel my heart speed up a bit and look away quickly.

"Hey?" Kevin says, and I look up just in time to see a cocky grin spread across his face. He looks down at his exposed chest through the shirt and then back up at me. "Are you checking me out, Alice Williams?" He laughs as I turn three different shades of red and leave him standing there, as I walk out of the barn.

I can still hear him laughing as I turn beside my parents' house and walk up my front porch.

I hear his boots crossing the gravel between us before I reach the door and then I feel his arms around me, lifting me off the boards under my feet and spinning me around to face him. He locks his lips to mine, and I feel every bit of me melt into him. I try to fight it, I really try. But I can't. The loneliness and emptiness inside of me washes away under his touch and I don't have the strength to push him away now.

He carries me inside and sits on the couch, never letting go of me or breaking our kiss. I'm sitting on his lap, straddling him and he's holding the back of my head, kissing me with every bit of desire that he's been holding back.

I feel him shift under me and know that this has to stop, right now, or we will both be in trouble.

"Dar..." I start to say, and he lets go of me instantly, pulling back and then moving me off him in one fell swoop. He's breathing heavily, and he's upset but trying not to show it.

"Oh Kevin, I'm so sorry" I tell him, putting my hand over his, but he pulls it out from under mine and stands up. "I just need a few minutes, Alley. I'll be back." He says and walks out the front door, getting into his truck, starting it and driving down the driveway, leaving me behind.

CHAPTER NINE

I'm still sitting on the couch when my phone starts to vibrate across the room from me on the table next to the recliner. I jump up, hoping to see Kevin's name, but it's Matt calling me instead.

"Hello?" I answer the phone, wondering what he would be calling me about. "Alice?" I hear Matt's frazzled voice coming from the other end and my heart falls to my feet. *Not again,* I think and feel my head start to go all fuzzy.

I sit down in the recliner and say, "Yeah, Matt, it's me. What's wrong, where's Kevin?" Not wanting to hear the answer.

"Kevin? I figured he was there with you. I'm calling about Joel." He says and I catch my breath. "He's awake, Alice! Jess wanted me to call to tell you and to ask if you'd come to the hospital."

All kinds of emotions come over me all at once. I'm relieved that he's not calling to tell me bad news about Kevin. I try to ignore the nightmares, but I guess they're affecting me more than I realize.

I'm overjoyed that Joel is awake and he's obviously doing well enough that they want me to come up there.

And I'm also horrified at the idea of walking into that hospital; the last place I ever saw or spoke to Darry. The place that now haunts my dreams, making me a total crazy person.

"Yeah, I'll be right there", I tell him, and head out the door, praying the whole way there that God will go into the hospital with me and not let me enter that place alone.

When I pull into the parking lot of the hospital, I can barely breathe. The anxiety overcomes me, and I am in a full-on panic attack before I ever even reach the door. My legs are wobbly, and I feel very unsteady, but I walk through the glass double doors anyway. Inside I know that I can steady myself on the rail that runs down the length of every corridor within the hospital. But falling is not my biggest worry, though it probably should be.

No, my biggest worry is making it down the same corridor that I see in my sleep, that causes me grief and makes me sick. I pick up my feet and like a robot, I force them to carry me down the hall in front of me, one foot at a time.

I hear Matt's voice booming down the hall before I'm even close to the room. To get to Joel's room, I realize I'll have to cross by the same room that Darry died in. The same room that I find myself in most nights recently, as soon as I drift off to sleep.

Realizing I won't be able to do this if I don't start running now, I let go of the rail and take off down the hall. I know people are staring and the nurses would probably be very upset with me and scold me... if they could catch me, but I don't care. I am determined not to let this get the best of me and I want to see Joel and know that he's ok.

Right as I'm passing Darry's room, Brittany steps out of Joel's and sees me running toward her. Her eyes go wide and her mouth opens as if she's going to say something, but I can't stop, I can't slow down. I run right by her into Joel's room and everyone stops talking to turn and look at me; out of breath, my chest heaving up and down. I bend over and lean on my knees, holding my belly with my free arm.

I didn't even see Kevin in the room, but he's by my side now, asking me if I'm ok, his arm around my back as he's bent down, pulling my hair back to look me in my face. I look over at him and smile, and all I can get out between heavy breaths is, "I'm good. I did it, Kevin. I got by his room."

I stand up and look at the bed in front of me. Joel is sitting up with Jessica sitting in a chair beside his bed, holding his hand. Matt and Brittany are standing by the large glass window and in the corner are Joel's mom, dad and sister. "Good thing these rooms are huge, huh?" I ask them all and they burst out laughing, thankful to break the tension brought into the room by my overly dramatic entrance just moments ago.

I smile at Kevin and he takes my hand, leading me over to an empty chair beside Jessica. "Sit down, please, before you give me a heart attack, woman." He takes his place behind me, putting his hands on both of my shoulders, massaging them gently.

Joel smiles up at us and I can see the light bruises that are starting to fade away. His cuts have all but healed and he seems to be doing fine. His head still has a bandage around it, so I can't exactly see what's going on there, but he seems alert and coherent enough to put me at ease over his well-being.

Joel points to my belly and says, "So, a girl, huh?" and winks at me. I nod and smile, holding my belly, I tell him, "Yeah, I know... a little Alice. Watch out world!" And everyone laughs again.

"I know that's right", Kevin says, and I turn to slap his arm. He bends down to kiss my cheek and I hear the breaths getting sucked in around the room and Jess shifting in the seat next to me, but no one says anything. And for that I'm grateful. I definitely don't want to try to explain something to someone else that I don't even understand yet myself. That is not a conversation that I'm ready to have just yet, but I know that Kevin and I need to talk about it, and soon. I silently pray that he's coming home with me as my belly begins to rumble loudly and I remember that I haven't eaten anything today.

"She's telling you that it's past time to feed her", Kevin says to me.

"Haven't you eaten anything, Alice?" Jessica asks me, looking concerned.

"Not yet, I kind of got sidetracked this morning before I had a chance." I say, blushing and I feel Kevin gently squeeze my shoulder.

"Let's go grab some breakfast then", Kevin says to me, gently lifting me up by my elbow. "Anyone else hungry?" He says, looking around the room at all of the faces staring at us like we suddenly have three heads each.

"Yeah, man, I could eat", Matt says turning to Brittany. "You hungry, dear?" She nods and we all say that we'll be right back and head toward the door. I stop to go back and hug Joel, who gives me a gentle squeeze and whispers in my ear, "Darry wouldn't mind, ya know." I pull back and look at him, confusion all over my face. He just winks at me and gives me a thumbs up with a joyful smile.

I leave the room and see Kevin has waited for me to come out. "I told them to go on down to the cafeteria and we'd meet them there. I hope you don't mind."

I shake my head and look down at my feet and Kevin's feet, and notice the sizable difference. He puts his hand under my chin, lifting my face to his and kisses the tip of my nose softly. "I'm sorry I ran out like that. I just didn't want you to see me upset. I know I don't have the right to be..."

"Yes! Yes, you do, Kevin. I had no right to call you by his name. I didn't mean to either, I hope you know that." I tell him. He nods, and says, "I do. That's what upset me."

CHAPTER TEN

The cafeteria downstairs is almost empty when we get there. We see Matt and Brittany sitting at a table, waiting for us, waving us over to them when we come through the door. I can see the question in their expressions as we approach the table.

I really don't want to have this conversation. I don't want to have to explain why or how Kevin and I have gotten so close with Darry being gone less than a month. I don't think I could if I tried.

And I know he doesn't want to have to explain how he loves me and how I can't return the same feelings for him but that I love him for being here for me. It sounds awful just saying it in my own head!

Oh, I'm a horrible person.

We all go to grab our food and I see that they have scrambled eggs and bacon... with toast. I grab my food and head over to the table to sit down when Brittany sits next to me, and asks, "So, what's going on with you and Kev?"

My shoulders drop and I look down at my plate, regretting coming to the hospital.

"Britt, if you don't mind, I really don't want to talk about it right now. I don't think I could give you a satisfactory explanation, anyway. I don't know myself, to be honest."

She nods and puts her arm around my shoulders giving me a gentle squeeze. "I understand. No problem. No judgments either, just so you know." She says, winking at me and taking a bite of the oatmeal in front of her.

Kevin and Matt walk over to us with plates piled high. "Wow! Did y'all leave anything for anyone else? You know it's bad to take food from sick people, right?" Brittany says, smirking at Matt.

"Man, there's plenty of food up there. This isn't anything, I'm planning on going back, watch..." Matt says, sitting down, leaning in to kiss Brittany's shoulder.

"It's not a buffet, Matt, geez", Brittany teases him and me and Kevin laugh with her. Kevin looks up at me and winks, giving me his best sexy smile. I hate this. I don't want to hurt him. He's been so good to me. I wish we could just go back. I can't imagine ever loving anyone the way I love Darry and seriously not less than a month after losing him. But I don't want to lose Kevin either. I know he's going to get sick of chasing someone that's too empty to give anything back. He will leave; it's not a matter of if, but of when.

The thought breaks my heart and I can't finish my breakfast. I wish I could give him what he needs just so he will stay.

I watch him sitting across from me, smiling and laughing, cutting up with Matt and just being silly. His eyes are so bright when he laughs, and his smile... it's probably my favorite one (other than Darry's, of course), it's just so beautiful and so incredibly sincere. His whole face lights up and you can't help but smile with him; the light that radiates from him pulls you in and you're overwhelmed by his beauty before you even know that you've been taken in by him.

But the best thing, the greatest part of him is how he soothes me by just being there. When I'm upset, or hurting so badly over missing Darry, he's there; he's always right there. When he wraps me in his arms, it doesn't fade away, but he makes everything more bearable. He calms me and my anxiety. I'm able to just melt into him and he engulfs me in such a way that I don't have to feel the rawness of my feelings alone anymore. He takes it all into him, letting me sink into his arms and allowing me to cry or scream into his chest if I need to. He doesn't try to stop me or tell me it'll be ok just so I will stop, instead he just lets me feel it and then he helps me move on from it.

That's the best thing that anyone could do for me. And I think he knows that.

"Alley, do you want to go shopping later today? I'm seriously chomping at the bit to buy adorable little girl clothes!" Brittany asks, hopeful that I will say yes.

I feel a small panic come over me and look from her to Kevin, unsure if I'm really up for shopping. "I... I don't know..." I start, feeling the anxiety begin to rise up. Kev reaches over and puts his hand on mine. "I will be there with you. We can go out of town to shop wherever you want, Alley. We don't have to stay around here", he says, calming me instantly. "I'd kind of like to go buy some things myself", he adds, smiling at me and leaning over to put his forehead to mine, "She is gonna need stuff."

I don't know what possesses me, but I tilt my head up and kiss him, like a real, serious kiss that says a lot more than just "Thank you", and the table goes completely silent for the duration of the kiss.

We just stare into each other's eyes for a moment and then he breaks the stare by turning toward Matt and Brittany, "Well... I don't really know how to explain that", he says, laughing nervously, as we both look at the gaping stares on our friends faces.

I just put my hands up to either side of me and shrug, tilting my head slightly to the side all I can do is give them an innocent smile and a nervous laugh. "I couldn't tell ya myself." I say, putting my hand over Kevin's and squeezing it.

"Alright then, where are we going?" Matt says, clapping his hands together, changing the subject, thankfully.

"Well, right now we're going back up to see Joel and Jess, but we'll talk about where to go shopping after", Britt tells him, standing to take her plate to the trashcan. Matt follows her, but Kev stays behind a second to look at me. Raising an eyebrow, his expression asking me about that kiss, I just smile and kiss his cheek, standing to throw my plate away. I turn to quickly follow behind our friends.

CHAPTER ELEVEN

Back in the room, Joel is resting, his family has left to go home, wanting to eat and clean up, but Jess is still right there. She's leaned over the bed, her head lying right beside him, her hand over his. They're so sweet together. It makes my heart hurt to see them there like this; for all they're going through and because I'm jealous. I don't wish anything bad on Joel and I'm so happy that he's going to be ok, but why couldn't Darry wake up too? Why did Darry have to leave us? It's not fair! God, why?!

I have to leave the room. I've got to get away from here. These thoughts are ugly and all consuming. I'm ashamed of myself for envying Jessica for having Joel here with her still and for being upset with Joel, Matt and Kevin too, for surviving when Darry didn't. I feel the tingle all over my body. The heat rising through me.

Without saying a word to anyone, I turn and run down the corridor to the parking lot, tears starting to stream down my face, feeling like I can't breathe.

I run all the way to the cemetery without stopping and fall on my knees in front of the small angel statue, placed in his memory. I'm out of breath and sobbing like crazy. Even outside, in the open, I feel claustrophobic, like the world is closing in around me. My skin is clammy, and my thoughts are scattered. My heart is beating so hard and so fast that it feels like it's going to break through my chest and fall on the ground before me.

When I catch my breath, I scream and punch my fists into the ground underneath me, hitting the earth below where I am now. I am suddenly so angry; it feels like fire coursing through my veins and I can't stop screaming. I scream over and over, as loud as I can, until it feels like my throat is going to bleed. I stand up and look up to the sky, my hands thrown up in defiance and I begin screaming at God. "Why, Lord?! Why?!" I demand answers from Him now. "Why would you give him to me and then turn around and take him away? I don't understand this! Please help me understand! This isn't fair!!" I scream at the top of my lungs at the invisible presence that I know is there because I can feel Him all around me.

I drop back to my knees, crying again, "Please... Lord. Please help me understand this. What are you doing here? I need your help; I can't do this on my own", I tell Him, in whispered defeat.

I hear footsteps approaching from behind me, but I don't have the strength to lift my head that now rests on the grass. I continue to cry, allowing my tears to soak into the earth beneath me; unable to care about how uncomfortable I am lying like this and praying for God to take my feelings away, all of them. I just want to be numb because being numb has to be better than this.

I feel someone lie down behind me and an arm slides under my head, lifting it up and off the hard ground, another over my body, pulling me back against someone's chest. My eyes close and I drift away, leaving the nightmare that is now my life.

I'm in a beautiful place with magnificent castles and majestic palaces in the clouds. A man dressed in white robes that seems to have a glow radiating from all around him, walks up to me and puts his arm out to me, locking arms we walk together along the fluffy white clouds. He smiles at me and every pain, every horrible emotion, every anxiety and worry falls off of me. The only thing left is an overpowering sense of peace and love. I smile back at him and I realize that I'm walking with God!

He doesn't say a word, He just continues to walk with me, never removing His arm from my shoulders and He keeps smiling at me. When we reach the end of the clouds, He winks at me and nudges my shoulder, allowing me to fall slowly and peacefully to the earth below us.

I wake with a jolt and sit up, a smile across my lips and a new sense of comfort and peace in my heart.

I look over beside me to see who's there, who slid their arm under me and hugged me until I fell asleep? And I see the sweetest face, sleeping so soundly, a small grin across his lips. Kevin is there; *he's always there.* I think and smile, laying back down and scooting into his arms.

He shifts beside me and opens his eyes, locking onto mine. "Hey there", he says with a sleepy grin. "This is an odd place to nap, yeah?" He puts his hand on my arm and runs it slowly up and down, soothing me and letting me know he cares for me, deeply. "How are you feeling?"

He asks, not asking what happened or why we ended up here. He simply wants to know that I'm ok and that warms my heart, making me feel an even stronger pull to him.

"I'm better now", I tell him. "but I don't know if I'll ever be the same." He pulls my head to his chest, smoothing the back of my hair and he kisses the top of my head. "I know, I don't think any of us will ever be the same again."

"Do you still want to go shopping?" He asks with hope in his voice. "Yeah, I think I'll be ok. I do think I want to leave this town though, too many memories here. I need to get out of here", I tell him right as Matt and Brittany pull up at the curb down the hill from where we are currently lying.

"They have impeccable timing, don't they?" He asks, smirking toward Matt's new Jeep. "Yeah, I think Matt can secretly read our minds", I tell him and laugh.

"I like that sound of that", Kevin says to me, sitting up and turning his body toward me. I sit up with him and look over at him, asking, "What? That Matt can read our minds?" the confusion showing in my tone. Kevin laughs and shakes his head, "No, silly girl. I like the sound of you laughing." He puts his arm around my shoulder and gives me a side hug. He stands in front of me at my feet and grabs both of my hands, pulling me up to stand in front of him. He hugs me, totally and completely engulfing me in his arms and I bury my head into his chest, taking in his wonderful scent.

He kisses my head and drops his arms, grabbing my hand to guide me down the hill toward the Jeep. "I won't tell you that everything's going to be ok, Alley, but I can promise you that I'll always be here for you and I'll help you in every way that you'll let me", he says to me before we make it over to our friends. He lifts my hand and brings it to his lips, kissing it and then helps me up into the Jeep, jumping in beside me and Matt takes off down the road, leading us out of town.

I feel the heaviness of everything I've been holding onto start to leave me; getting further and further from my mind with each passing mile. With the wind blowing through my hair, I feel at ease, throwing my arms up over my head, to let them feel the pressure of the wind and the freedom of the growing distance between me and that town.

CHAPTER TWELVE

Pulling into the large mall parking lot, I realize just how long it's been since I've been here. I had forgotten how massive this place really is. Everything in Cedar Ridge is small and humble in comparison. I'm not used to seeing such intimidating buildings and crowds like what's surrounding us now.

Kevin jumps out of the Jeep and reaches in to take my hand, "Ready to go do this?" he asks, nodding toward the mall. "Yes sir!" I assure him and step down out of the vehicle.

Matt and Brittany are right beside us, holding hands and smiling over at us, "Let's go buy baby stuff!!" she says, excitedly. "I'm buying her a football jersey", Matt informs me, and Kevin laughs when Brittany pops Matt in the arm, telling him, "You are not! Dallas is going to have ballerina shoes and pink tutus, not football jerseys and cleats!"

Matt reaches the door first, opening it and holding his arm out, saying, "entrer", with a fake French accent. He lets each of us pass before stepping in and allowing the door to close behind us.

The mall is cooler than I expected, giving me goosebumps as soon as we walk in. "Do you want me to go back for my jacket?" Kevin asks when he sees me rubbing my arms to warm them. "No, it's ok. I'll adjust but thank you."

The store is full of baby stuff, but nothing that I really like. We walk out of this store and into the main part of the center of the mall and look for other baby stores to explore. When we go inside of the next one, Kevin excuses himself and leaves us to go do something while me and Britt search through racks and racks of baby girl clothes. Matt walks over to the sports themed baby clothes, staying true to his word as he searches for my baby girl's first football jersey.

Brittany and I find loads of adorable clothes and toss them into the little buggy we somehow managed to grab up before someone else took it; it was the last one as far as we could tell.

She finds her pink baby tutu and a tiny little bubblegum pink body suit to go with it. "See, I told you, baby ballerina." She says, smiling, happy with her find.

Kevin comes over to us; walking up behind me, he wraps his arms around me, leaning his chin on my shoulder, looking over me at the clothes in front of us. "Do you think that's enough clothes to start her with?" He asks sarcastically. "I think we're gonna need bigger closets." He says, laughing.

I shake my head, again, at his choice of words... "*we're gonna need?*"

"Yeah, I guess you're right, we should probably stop now." I say, looking at Brittany who was just about to drop another tiny outfit into the buggy but stops flat and then let's go anyway, dropping it, still maintaining eye contact with Kev, who closes his eyes and shakes his head.

He lifts his chin from my shoulder and spins me around to face him, wrapping his arms around my waist and pulling me to him, the only space between us created by my baby bump.

"I got her some things too. They'll be delivered tomorrow afternoon-ish", he tells me.

Matt comes back to us carrying an arm full of stuff. He tosses in a plush football and baseball, a black and red jersey and tiny shoes that look like little baby cleats, studs and all, of course. "Are you kidding me, Matthew Norton?!" Britt says sternly, putting her hand on her hip.

"You're calling me out by my name, really?" He says, shaking his head, dropping the cleats down into the buggy dramatically. "No, I'm not kidding you. She'll need these when she's making touchdowns in her crib!" He turns to walk to the checkout, not another word spoken.

Kevin shrugs his shoulders and we make our way behind Matt to pay for everything.

The bags fill the only empty spaces around us all, in the Jeep. We pull out of the parking lot and I lean my head onto Kevin's shoulder, enjoying the feel of the breeze blowing my hair around my face. "Pppbblllttttt!" I turn to see Kevin working hard to get my hair out of his face, laughing the whole time.

"Oh, sorry", I tell him, pulling my hair into a ponytail with a band that I had around my wrist. "Better?" I ask and he nods, "Much."

Matt and Britt drop us off at our vehicles in the hospital parking lot, telling us they're headed back up for a while. They'll text to let us know how he's doing. A twinge of guilt starts to pull at me as I remember the horrible thoughts from earlier. I do my best to push them aside and walk over to my car, loading it with bags.

When we get home, in front of the door is a beautifully wrapped package. The white paper has little pink hearts all over it and it's all tied up in a big pink satin bow. All the card says is, "Dallas Williams."

"I wonder who this is from", I say to Kevin as he opens the door, and grab the package to bring it in with us. "It's kind of heavy", I tell him, and he grabs it from me. "Yeah, it is."

We take the package to the couch and I open it. I stand back, staring at it, not sure what to say or feel. It's beautiful and I know instantly who sent it. "I'll be right back, Kev", I tell him as I turn to leave. Outside, I hurry down the steps and turn off into the trees to the left of my house. I follow the path to the house next door and walk up to the front door. I don't knock, I just walk in and search for the person that I need to see.

"Bobby? Are you here?" I call out into the house. Dishes clank together and fall to the floor in the kitchen.

"Yeah, I'm back here!" He calls out to me and I walk into the kitchen to see him bent down picking up the bowls he dropped.

He stands up and looks at me as I cross the room to throw my arms around his neck. He hugs me and says, "Whoa, whoa... What's this about?" Trying to act like he didn't leave the package at my door.

"I know it was you, Bobby. You're the only one that had that photograph of us", I tell him. "Thank you. It's absolutely perfect!"

"Well, you're very welcome", he says, blushing from the unwanted attention.

"Well, I'm gonna get back to my lunch then", he says, dismissing himself so he can break away from the awkwardness he feels from the recognition that he wasn't expecting.

I hug him and thank him again but he just smiles at me and turns to the stove. I leave the house eager to get back to the gift, wondering where it will go.

When I enter the house, I step through the door to go into the livingroom and the frame is gone. The wrapping paper and bow have all been removed too. "Kevin?" I call into the house. "Where's the frame?" I wait to hear him call back to me.

He walks in the room, a towel wrapped around his waist and another drying his hair. My eyes travel up and down the length of his body and I feel the blood rush to my cheeks. When I make eye contact with him again, he's got a sexy smirk across his face, "Enjoying me, are you?" He steps into the room and comes over to me, bending down to kiss my cheek. "You don't have to blush, Alley. I know I'm hot", he teases, and I smack him in the side. The sound of the slap rings through the room as the pink welt rises up on him immediately. "Geez! No need for such violence." He cries, wincing against the sting, and coming after me.

I put my hands up to stop him, pushing against his chest, but he easily pushes through my resistance and wraps his arms around me, biting my neck, playfully.

I feel the heat rush through my body and pull away quickly.

CHAPTER THIRTEEN

"Oh, wow! Um... not sure I'm ready for that just yet..." I say to him, turning to go sit across the room. I look up at him expecting to see a look of disgust, anger or frustration, anything except for the look of amusement that's now all over his face.

He grins and leans forward; resting one elbow on his knee, one hand pinching his chin and the other he lifts to run through his messy blonde hair. "So, what you're saying is... in time..." And he gazes up at me, clearly loving how he makes me squirm in my seat.

"Kevin!" I laugh nervously at his cocky demeanor and he leans forward lowering himself to his knees on the floor in front of the couch. He moves slowly across the carpet, never breaking eye contact. When he makes it to me, he raises himself up, putting his hands on either side of my knees and lifts his face to mine.

He kisses me again, this time soft and sweet, the side of his thumb tracing gently down the line of my jaw and then under my chin. He pulls back and whispers oh so softly into my ear, "I love you, Alley. Ready or not."

His tone and choice of wording takes me back instantly to when we were all kids playing hide and seek on the playground. I remember running and laughing, playing along with everyone. I remember Darry calling my name and saying he'll find me, warning me that I can't hide from him. And then another old and long-lost memory pops into my head, something that I'd forgotten about until hearing Kevin say those words to me just now. I'm pulled back in time, Kevin and I are hiding from Darry behind the big gray electric box. Darry's counting and then we hear him say, "Ready or not, here I come", just then Kevin leans over me, taking my face into his hands, he kisses me and whispers to me, "I love you, Alice. I'll always love you." And he gets up and runs out from behind the box, letting Darry tag him.

"Oh, Kevin..." I whisper. "You kissed me and told me you loved me...when we were just kids, playing hide and seek on the school playground."

His eyes fly open wide and then he just grins at me. I watch as the memory flashes back into his mind. "I told you I've always loved you." He smiles, "What? You didn't believe me?" He asks, raising his eyebrow and leaning in to kiss me again. Then, bringing his lips right to my ear, he whispers softly, "I told you then, I'll always love you, Alice."

I put my hand to the side of his face and move his lips to mine. I pull him closer to me and throw my arms around his neck. He lays me back in the recliner, bringing his body to hover over mine, supporting his weight on his arms. He kisses me again and then pulls himself back to sit on his legs. I sit up to look him in his eyes, seeing by his expression exactly where his thoughts had just been.

His face is flushed, and his chest is rising and falling faster than normal. I can see the desire in his eyes, but something is holding him back. I see the struggle happening inside of him.

"Alley, I really want to be with you. I mean... I reeeeeaaallllly want to. But I can't. Not like this. Not right now." He looks down, and when he looks up again, I see the angish in his eyes, the pain very evident in his expression. "Man, Alley. I wish you knew how much I love you. How badly I want to be here with you. Not just here *for* you, but *with* you." My hearts races at his words. "...but I can't. It isn't right. One day though... when you really want *me*. When you're ready to have *me*."

He pats my knee and excuses himself, walking into the kitchen. I hear the refrigerator door open and close and then a chair squeaks as it's being pulled out and then in again. I hear the glass being placed on the table and then I hear the deep, sorrowful sigh escape from Kevin.

My heart breaks and honestly, I have to pull myself together. I was certainly ready to let him act as Darry would have. What is wrong with me?! Darry is still all over me. He's barely gone, and I was ready to let Kevin do things to me that Darry would kill us both over. Ugh!

I walk into the kitchen. Kevin is sitting at the table in the dark, but the light coming in through the window illuminates the room just enough for me to make out his silhouette. He's leaned over the table resting his head in his hands. "I think I need to leave for a while." He says to me, not turning or moving his head from his hands. And I panic. I go over to him, kneeling down beside him, I put my hand on his leg and look up into his sad eyes, begging him not to go. I plead with him not to leave me alone as tears stream down my cheeks.

"Alice, I'm not doing this to hurt you. I just need time to think." He says, standing up, scooting the chair out behind him. He slowly pushes it back under the table, and turns to walk out of the room, leaving me standing there all alone in the kitchen. Unable to move or speak. I hear him moving around the house, getting dressed and collecting his keys. I hear him walk out the front door, closing it behind him, and I fall to my knees in the middle of the kitchen floor, sobbing.

I listen as he pulls out of the driveway and onto the street, driving away from me, putting me behind him as nothing more than an unwanted memory.

CHAPTER FOURTEEN

The next day I wake up still lying in the middle of the kitchen floor. I hear a knock at the door and then another one and another one. I walk to the door and look out to see two men in uniforms, each propping up a large box in front of them. "Can I help you?" I call through the door.

"Yes, ma'am, we have a delivery for a Mrs. Alice Williams." He says, looking down at his clipboard.

I open the door and see that the boxes have pictures on them. One is a beautiful white circular crib with a white curtain draped around the top of it, like a canopy. The other box is a matching white changing table with a door on the right side of it; a tiny little closet just for hanging the baby's clothes in.

My heart sinks and I know that this is what Kevin was talking about. He ordered these for Dallas.

I step aside, allowing the men to bring the boxes in. They set them down in the foyer just before the kitchen and turn to leave, wishing me a good day and congratulating me on the baby.

I close the door and walk over to the boxes, looking closer at the photos, tracing my hand along each one. I sit down on the floor in front of them, and just stare, wondering how I got here. How my life turned into this big nasty mess.

I'm eighteen, widowed, pregnant and alone.

I just managed to run off the one person that has been here for me nonstop, comforting me and making me feel half normal again. Not that my family and Darry's family hasn't been here too, it's just... different.

I hear the front door open and close and look over to see my daddy coming into the house. He comes over and sits down beside me, putting his hand on my knee, patting it. "What do you have there, sweet pea?" He asks, smiling a half smile at me, and pointing to the boxes in front of me. "Need help with it?"

I nod and lean my head over to lay it on his shoulder and he drops his head on mine. "Rough night?" He asks and stops, sensing that he shouldn't pry any further. "You could say that", I tell him and lift my head.

"I don't know what I'm doing wrong, Daddy. I feel so split down the middle, you know? On the one hand, I just said goodbye to my husband; my one and only very best friend in the whole world. I have only ever known Darry, Daddy. Now Kevin is here and Darry's not. And I can't change that. I can't take it back, as badly as I want him here, he will never be here again." I cry, small sobs beginning to burn in my chest.

"I feel like if I let myself move on this soon... if I allow myself to love Kevin and let him in, let him help me and be here for me and Dallas, I am somehow betraying Darry and our marriage, our love... his memory. But I don't want Kevin to leave either, Daddy. I do love him. As much as I don't want to, I can't help myself from feeling love toward him. It's not the same as my love for

Darry, I don't think anything can ever match that love, but it's still love."

He listens and allows me to finish and then he pulls me back by my shoulders and looks me in my eyes. "Baby, I knew and loved Darry too. And if there is anything that I knew about that boy, it's how much he loved you and always only wanted to make you happy and for you to feel safe. Darry isn't up there glaring down at you, seething at you for loving his best friend. Baby, he's smiling and overjoyed that you aren't alone here, hurting and making yourself sick. He's happy that Kevin is the one here taking care of his family for him, Alley. I know he is. He loved Kevin too. He would be thrilled to know that someone he loved and trusted is going to be here for his girls."

He hugs me to him and finishes by saying, "Alley, don't let yourself miss out on another wonderful love because you're worried that the first one will somehow be tainted by it. Darry wouldn't want that."

I try to give him my best smile, but it falls short and he laughs gently at the attempt. "Do you know where he is? Is he coming back?" I shake my head and he nods. "Well... do you want to put these together now or do you want to wait?" He asks, pointing to the boxes.

"Can we wait a little while, please?" I ask him, not wanting to open the boxes without Kevin. It just doesn't feel right.

"Sure, sweetheart, but you better not wait too long. Our

girl will be here very, *very* soon." He says, touching my belly just as Dallas kicks against it. His face lights up and he says, "Oh, wow! I remember when it was you kicking me like that. Seems like it was just yesterday. Time sure does fly."

He gets up to leave but before he does, he turns to me, standing in the open doorway, he says, "Don't let him get too far gone, Alley. If you love him... tell him. Before it's too late." And with that said, he turns and closes the door behind him, leaving me with a lot to think about.

Is he right? Could he be right about how Darry would be ok with me and Kevin, and so soon? And why is no one else as put off about the idea as I am? Even Brittany and Matt didn't seem too bothered or shocked even. I mean yeah, they were surprised, but they didn't seem upset or judgmental in any way.

I go to find my phone and realize it's not anywhere in any part of the house that I'm usually in. And then it hits me; Kevin charges it at night for me... in my bedroom. Understanding what this means, I have to take a few minutes to sit and wrap my head around going into that room, and I have to do it alone.

I sit on the couch and look into the room first, trying to talk myself into it. I need my phone. I want to text him, to call him, to plead with him to come home. But I have to talk myself into it first. I sit there in the livingroom for at least twenty minutes trying to convince myself to get up and then arguing with myself over how silly I'm being.

Finally, I get up and cross the space from the couch to the door and I stand there for a few minutes. I flip the light switch and look around the room that seems so unfamiliar now. Right away I notice that Kevin has come in here and taken down all of the photos of me and Darry. There's not a single one left. It hurts a bit to see them gone, but I know it's better this way, especially tonight.

I step into the room and walk over to sit down on my side of the bed. The room feels smaller, less inviting than it once felt. But the urge to run and hide away from it has faded. I keep thinking back to that dream in the cemetery and how I felt afterward. And then thinking of my daddy's words to me; I feel like a weight has been lifted. I know that he's right, Darry loved me, and he would understand the hows and whys of how me and Kevin have grown so close.

I will never be able to give my heart to someone the same way I did to Darry, and that's just a fact, something that I cannot help. He knew me in ways that no one will ever know me again. We shared every moment of our lives together for such a long time, that we had already lived a lifetime together before we were married.

But I love Kevin too, and I need him, and I believe he needs me too. I know that Dallas will need him and love him. If he comes back home, she won't know anything but Kevin, from day one.

I reach for my phone and pick it up, silently praying that he has called or sent a text to check on me... but he hasn't.

I open my messages and find his name waiting there at the top, staring at me, begging me to reach out. So, I do.

Kevin, where are you? We need to talk. Please.

I wait a few minutes, praying that he will answer me. After what feels like forever, he finally answers.

Are you ok? I'm at my parents' house. I'll head that way in a few minutes, I was just talking with my mom.

Yeah, I'm ok. I just need to talk to you. It's nothing bad. Just come when you can. I'll be here.

His response fills me with hope, maybe I haven't lost him after all. But I know that this is a very fragile situation and if I don't get it together, I could possibly lose him too. The thought of losing someone else hurts so bad. I lay back on my pillow and pull my legs in against my body and allow myself to drift off to sleep, refusing to let myself sit here and stew until he gets here.

I wake up to my hair being swept off of my face and lips pressing to my forehead. "Wake up, sleepyhead", a voice says to me, calling me out of my peaceful slumber. "Huh? Kevin?" I ask, trying to get my eyes to concentrate on the face in front of me. When his gorgeous green eyes come into focus, I smile and relax. I close my eyes and let everything pour out of me, "Kevin. I'm so glad you came back to me. I want you to move in here, *with* me, please. I love you, Kev, I need you here with me. Please say you'll come back home."

His mouth begins to turn up at the edges as he leans in and kisses me. He sits back, bringing his hand to his mouth and resting it on his bottom lip, a grin forming behind it. "You thought I left you, like never coming back left you? And you were worried?" he asks, and I can tell he's liking this... too much.

I whine at him and pout my lips, giving him my best sad eyes, I turn away from him so he can't see my face, and bury it in the pillows. "Ohhhhh no! You're not getting away from me, Alley! Tell me what you thought."

I throw a small hissy fit into the bed, kicking my legs and bouncing my butt up in the air. I hear him laughing at me, so I grab the pillow under me and turn to smack him with it, but I hit him harder than I expected to, and he flies backwards off the bed. I jump up and kneel down beside him apologizing emphatically. "I'm so so sorry, Kev! I didn't mean to knock you off the be..." But he's pulled me down onto him now and he's kissing me.

"Wait a minute, Kevin. We need to talk first", I tell him, pleading with him to understand.

He gets up and sits beside me on the bed. "Ok, let's talk, but first I want you to know something... I was never going to leave you, Alice. I just needed to get away for a while, to clear my head. I needed to talk to my mom, and I needed you to have time to think as well. I told you I wouldn't leave until you told me to, and we see how that worked out... the one time you told me to leave, I slept on the porch, I mean come on." He reaches down and picks up my hand, bringing it to his lips, he looks me in the eyes and kisses my knuckles. "I'm not going anywhere. I'm here for the duration, if you'll have me. I love you. There's nowhere I'd rather be."

I look at him, his expression all serious and I put my hand to his face, trying to be just as serious and I ask him, "So, what you're saying is, I'm not going to get rid of you that easily?" And he laughs, pulling me in for another kiss. "That's *exactly* what I'm saying."

CHAPTER FIFTEEN

I wake up and reach over for Kevin but he's not there. The bed beside me is empty, but I know he's here.

We've actually slept in the bed every night for the past few months. I haven't had a single nightmare and I haven't broken down once!

I hear Kevin moving around in the kitchen and the smell of coffee brewing draws me out of the room. I walk into the kitchen and see him wearing my black apron and I can't help but laugh so hard my stomach starts hurting. My apron is black with tiny pink hearts all over it and it's got pink frills running along both sides.

"What? You don't like my fashion statement?" He says, holding the spatula out to the side and looking down at the apron and back up at me. "I'm not getting bacon grease all over me and I am not too good to wear pink hearts and frills." He says turning back to the stove.

"Sit down and breakfast will be right up."

I look around and this guy has scrambled eggs, toast, jelly and butter, cut up pieces of cantaloupe and orange juice already on the table. "You know... you're kind of awesome", I tell him, smiling at him shaking his booty back and forth as he flips the bacon over in the frying pan.

"Yeah, so I've been told", he says, smirking at me over his shoulder.

"Humble too", I quip back.

I pick up a piece of toast and start buttering it and slapping blueberry jelly on it too. "I'm starving! And this all smells so delicious!" I tell him, grabbing two spoonfuls of scrambled eggs. "Ok, I'm ready for the bacon now, can't you hurry it along or something?" I ask, teasing him.

"Coming right up, my dear", he says as he turns to put the bacon on my plate. "Thank you, sir."

He comes around to sit next to me, filling his plate too. We begin eating and he tells me he's been up since 4am, putting together the crib and the changing table, which are both now neatly and safely in the nursery. Which is good because I'm only two weeks away from my due date and have been told by my doctor that she'd be surprised to see me go another week.

I've already started to dilate; I can feel the shift in the baby's position and the pressure that's now on my lower abdomen. I've been using the bathroom a lot because of this change, and I've been having some Braxton Hicks contractions, which scared the holy hallelujah out of us the first few times. We had grabbed the hospital bag and run out of the house, headed to the hospital twice in the middle of the night, only to be checked out and sent back home again. It was embarrassing but also necessary seeing as neither of us have any idea what we're doing or what to expect as far as real actual labor.

"I want to see what you've been doing in there, Kevin. Can I please come in and take a look now?" I whine at him, begging him and giving him my best sad puppy dog eyes.

"Yes, ma'am, I believe it's ready for you now."

He'd said the nursery was off limits for the past few days. Ever since the baby shower, last Saturday, he refused to let me in. He said he wanted to surprise me. I'm so stinkin excited to see what he's been doing; it's been hard not to take a peak while he's working on the farm with my dad.

I finish up my breakfast and start to get up to go check it out when he grabs me by the waist and pulls me down on his lap, moving my hair and kissing the back of my neck, he tells me, "Not so fast! I want to see you when you see it." He gets up, lifting me up with him and we walk into the hallway.

Kevin goes first, opening the door, bringing his hand around to flip the light switch on. He steps in and lets me pass into the room.

I look around at the colors and the cute mint green furry rug on the floor in front of the beautiful crib he bought for her. Then I see the changing table and the little stuffed lamb that Elaine bought her, sitting on the table.

The room is all pale pink and mint green, with a little white here and there. The white rocking chair that my mom and daddy bought me is tucked in the corner, the cushion on the chair is pale pink and so is the cushion on the rocking ottoman that sits in front of it. There's a table in front of the window with a beautiful white lamp that has little baby lambs all over it, the lamp shade is mint green with little white polka dots all over it.

It's all so gorgeous and I love everything he's done in this room. But when I turn to look at the crib and see the white edges of a frame peaking from behind the curtain, my breath catches, and my eyes go wide. I look from the frame to Kevin and back again, walking over to push the curtain back all the way, there on the wall is the framed photo collage that Mr. Williams had left on my front porch. In the center is a sonogram photo of Dallas, that I can only guess Kevin gave to him. It's the one that says, "It's a girl!!" To the top left of that is a baby picture of Darry and to the top right, a baby picture of me.

Underneath the sonogram photo is a picture of me and Darry, dancing our first dance at our wedding, but it was a special one because it was taken up close, right when he had leaned in to kiss me. I remember Bobby taking the photo because of the flash shocking us out of the kiss and the way Darry had laughed at the look on my face. It was a very sweet memory of our special night. I was grateful that Bobby had taken the photo and even more grateful that he had done this for me and Dallas... and Darry. The photos were all placed just so, when you look at them standing back, they form a heart. At the top of the frame the words, "I'll love you, forever" are boldly displayed in soft pink letters that really stand out against the white background.

"Thank you, Kevin. Thank you so much for hanging this here. I think you picked the perfect place for it." I tell him, hugging his neck, fighting back the tears. "You made this room beautiful. Dallas will love it just as much as I do, I'm sure of it. We're both so lucky to have you."

He kisses me and walks over to open her closet door, showing me all of her pretty dresses and sweaters hanging neatly, just waiting to be worn. He has her tiny little shoes lined up straight and in a row on the shelf above the dresses. And on the floor of the closet are bags and bags of diapers and baby wipes that people had brought to the shower. There are bags in every size from newborn and up. "We won't have to buy diapers, like ever!" I tell him and he nods in agreement.

When we're finished looking at the room we turn to leave and walk into the hall. I've almost reached the foyer and ready to go into the livingroom when I feel something wet run down my leg. I don't understand what's happening at first, and then it hits me. "Kevin! I've either just peed myself or my water just broke!" I scream out in a full-on panic. I'm standing in the hallway, my legs bent open, looking down at the puddle of water below me, not knowing what to do and not wanting to move in case the baby falls out.

Kevin grabs the bag and then he grabs me and carries me out the door, not phased one bit by my wet clothing touching him. He starts the car and takes off down the driveway, honking the horn over and over as we pass my parents' house. My dad sticks his head out of the barn and sees us flying down the gravel path, dirt flying up all around us. Daddy throws down the towel he's holding and runs for his truck calling my mom to come on. My dad puts it in drive just as Robby jumps into the back seat of the truck and they are soon right behind us.

"We have to call Darry's parents and your parents and Matt, and Brittany, and Jessica and Joel..." I start listing off names, anxiety overtaking me. Kevin pats my knee and says, "It's ok, babe, I've got it under control. We have a system, remember? Your mom is calling Darry's parents right now, and Elaine will notify my parents who will then call everyone else. It's ok, you just breathe and try to relax... we're about to meet our girl!" He says, grinning from ear to ear like a proud daddy.

My heart aches for a minute at the thought of Darry missing this. The tears come but I refuse to let Kevin see me cry over this right now. He's just as much her daddy, he's been here the whole pregnancy. He's done everything that Darry would have gladly done for his daughter and me but couldn't be here to do. Kevin is her daddy too. He deserves to have this moment.

CHAPTER SIXTEEN

By the time we get to the hospital, my contractions are coming closer and closer and getting more intense. I'm huffing and puffing, doing my very best breathing, but the pain is almost unbearable. Kevin's face is dark with concern, as he swoops me up in his arms, carrying me through the glass double doors.

"I need someone over here, now please!" He calls out to the empty nurse's station. "Hello?!"

A dark-haired lady comes out of the room behind the desk, a look of annoyance on her face. When she sees us, her expression changes and she's around the desk in a second getting a wheelchair. Kevin sits me in the chair and the nurse wheels me toward the elevators. My parents come running through the door just in time to see us go into the elevator and then the doors close.

She takes us up to labor and delivery, bringing me around to another nurse's station to sign me in. Kevin gives them the information that they need, and I'm wheeled into a room.

My mom comes in the door right behind us, out of breath and red faced. "Did you just run all the way up here?" Kev asks her. She bends down and rests on her knees for a second, holding her finger up to tell him to wait just a minute. "I... ran... up... the stairs."

She waits another minute and finishes, "Your dad and Robby are coming up the elevator, I couldn't wait." She walks over to the other side of the room and sits down in a chair while the nurse helps me onto the bed and starts hooking me up to monitors.

Kevin stands at the foot of the bed, watching and waiting for the nurse to leave so he can crawl into the bed beside me. As soon as she leaves, he does just that, letting me lean into him. I'm so happy when they bring the epidural into the room and check me again telling me it's almost time to push; a few more minutes and my doctor will be here to take over.

I'm nervous about pushing her out. I can't quite wrap my head around the thought of pushing a baby the size of a watermelon through my tiny little body and it's kind of freaking me out. As it gets closer and closer to time, I get more and more scared and start to cry into Kevin's shoulder. My mom and Elaine are here in the room with us and they're instantly by my side, comforting me, wiping the hair back from my sweaty forehead and rubbing my legs.

I look at my mom and whisper, "I'm so scared, Mom." She bends down real close and looks me right in my eyes and tells me, "So was I, baby, so was I. But it's not anything that women haven't been doing forever, and when she's here, the pain of it all will slide away as soon as you look into her beautiful, tiny little eyes." She kisses my forehead and the door opens. I expect to see my daddy or Mr. Williams, who are waiting in the waiting room with Robby and Beth and Kevin's parents, but it's my doctor, all dressed out, ready to deliver our baby girl into this world.

"I'm not ready yet, doc", I tell her, and she smiles at me, saying, "Well, sweetheart, ready or not, here she comes." She smiles at me sympathetically and says, "You can do this. I'm here and all of them are here for you too, we can do this."

She pulls the sheet up and tells me to scoot to the foot of the bed. Kevin gets up and stands beside the bed, a look of total fear in his eyes.

The nurse grabs my foot and puts it in the stirrup, then does the same with the other one. I am totally exposed in this room right now in front of all these eyes, and I can't bring myself to care. The pressure is so overwhelming and the urge to push starts taking over me. "Alice, not yet... wait a minute." The doctor tells me, and I didn't even realize I was bearing down.

The doctor is at my feet now, all I see is the top of her head as she "checks my progress."

"Oh, wow. Ok! We're moving now! We're about to deliver your baby girl!" She says, excitedly. "Push, Alice, just like your using the bathroom." Kevin is holding my hand as I bear down and give it everything I've got. I feel what can only be described as an intense pop and Kevin's eyes go wide. The doctor smiles up at me and stands up, kicking the chair away, pushing it behind her. She reaches down and hollers to me, "One more, Alice, give me a good one!" I push as hard as I can and feel the pain shoot into my head and then a release from the bottom half of me.

"Oh, my God!" Kevin cries. "She's absolutely beautiful, Alley! Just like her mommy." He says and reaches down to kiss me.

My mom and Elaine are holding each other's hands, crying, staring at their bloody and messy granddaughter, who has a head full of dark curls, just like her daddy.

They bring her beside the bed for me to look at her and then they take her to clean her up. When she's all clean they put her on my chest and she looks up at me with her tiny little eyes, questioning me as she's moving her little fingers by her face. The nurse tells me to try and let her latch, so I put her mouth to me, and she gets it right away.

Kevin is on the bed with us again, one of his arms over my head and the other over me, running his fingers over her hair. "Man, she's got his hair, doesn't she?" He says, all the love in the world in his expression as he looks at her. "He's here, ya know. He sees her, Alley, I know he does." He bends down and kisses her fat little cheeks. "I love you, so much, Alice." He kisses me and adds, "I love you too, you beautiful little girl." And she wraps her finger around his, holding tight to her daddy.

I fall asleep as she's nursing and when I wake up, she's gone. I panic, looking around to find her and see Kevin asleep next to me in the bed. I sit up and look around until I see my daddy, Mr. Williams and everyone else; my mom, Elaine, Kevin's parents, Matt, Britt, and Jess, all sitting by the window on the long couch that runs the length of the wall. Daddy's holding Dallas, she's dressed in a little pink gown that's drawn closed at the feet and she has a pink hat on her head. He's staring down into her tiny red face, cooing and talking to her in his best baby voice. I lay back and watch them all, not saying a word, not wanting to disturb the scene before me.

Everyone is gathered around her, this precious child of ours, all of ours, and I feel myself wishing for Darry. My heart tugging at his memory. *I wish you were here to hold our daughter, babe. She's beautiful. Please watch over her.*

I feel Kevin move and look over at him to see his eyes open, watching them the same as me. "Look at them with her." He says to me, quietly. "Look at all that love and adoration."

I nod and smile at him, and he adds, "She's one lucky little girl." And I know exactly what he means. She has the love and support of so many people that loved Darry and that love me and Kevin and now her too. I know immediately that she's going to be not only loved tremendously, but she's going to be seriously spoiled! And I'm perfectly ok with that.

CHAPTER SEVENTEEN

The first days home with Dallas were a total circus. Neither Kevin nor I had any idea what we were doing, and I was so thankful for everyone that came to help us. My mom, Darry's mom, and Kevin's mom took turns on a rotating schedule; so, did Brittany and Jessica. The guys would all come in for holding time too, but the big helpers as far as meals, cleaning and baby aid, were the women.

She's been home for three weeks now, and we're just really starting to feel settled in. We haven't even really had a chance to think about getting ready for Christmas. It's a lot tougher having a baby here to care for, but I appreciate the distraction, as it doesn't leave much time to think about the utter sadness that has taken up residence in my heart over Darry's death and him not being here for this. I still think of him, how could I not? I see him every time I look into her beautiful little face. And I still have my moments, when I feel like I can't breathe. During those times, I have to hand her to Kevin so I can go sit outside and cry or just to clear my mind.

But the constant unbearable ache that was there, has been overshadowed by my intense love for our daughter and the fact that she keeps me moving; my thoughts consumed with caring for her and making sure she has everything she needs.

My favorite time of day, is in the evenings, when it's just the three of us in our room and Kevin has her lying on the bed in front of him, his legs spread out on either side of her and he's just enjoying quiet time with her. He plays baby pat-a-cake with her, holding her tiny little hands in his and bringing them together as he whispers the rhyme to her. Or he'll just talk to her in his best baby voice, while she concentrates on his face, trying to make sense of him. Dallas loves him so much. And he adores her too. I'm thrilled that they have each other.

We're in the bed now; I'm all tucked in on my side, ready to fall out but they're both wide awake. Kevin's mom is staying here with us tonight. I can hear her in the livingroom watching some sitcom on the tv, every now and then she'll laugh quietly, trying not to disturb the baby. Kevin and Dallas are having their nightly play date, he tickles her gently and her eyes go wide as she squirms under his hands. Her expressions are hilarious, and Kevin laughs, completely taken by her. I put my hand on his shoulder and run it down his back, he looks over at me, still holding her hands in his, "You ready to go to sleep?" I ask him, more pleading than asking really.

"Yeah, ok. I'll put her in her bassinet", He tells me, standing up and lifting her from the bed. Her bassinet sits beside Kevin's side of the bed, where she's slept since we brought her home, unless she ends up falling asleep on his chest or mine. But not tonight. I'm exhausted and I don't wanna risk not waking up if I need to with her in the bed.

"Thank you", I tell him, giving him a very weak and tired smile.

He lays her down on her side and pulls a receiving blanket over her. She's in a zip-up footie pajama, so the thin blanket is enough to keep her comfy and cozy.

When Kevin comes back to the bed, he crawls one knee at a time toward me, with a look on his face that says he's not as tired as I am. He hovers over me, wearing only pajama pants, his chest exposed and his arms flexing while they support his weight. He leans down to kiss my lips, as he pulls my hair back, moving his way down to my neck, he nips at the skin and runs his hand down my bare arm.

I lean back against my pillows, totally exhausted but loving his soft, gentle touch and the smell of his skin. He always smells so wonderful, like a dark and spicy chocolate patchouli. I know it's the remnants of his body spray, but I love how it smells when it's starting to fade a bit and the natural scent of his skin starts to mix with it.

He drops back suddenly and leaves the bed, going out the door, moving things around in the livingroom. He comes back in and sits down next to me on the bed, smiling at me and he grabs my hand dropping something in it and then he closes my fingers over the cold, round object. I open my hand and see a little silver ring with diamonds set into the band. My eyes go wide and then my expression goes blank.

"Calm down, Alley, I'm not proposing", he says, reading my reaction accurately. "This is just a little something that I bought to show you that I want to propose, one day. I want this ring to be a reminder of how much I love you, and that I'm here for you, always. One day I will ask you to marry me, Alley. I hope when that time comes, you will say yes, but until then, I hope you'll let me continue to love you and just lay here with you, holding you and kissing your sweet lips. And I hope you'll love me back."

I slip the ring on my right ring finger and lay my head on his shoulder. "Thank you, Kevin, it's gorgeous, and such a sweet gesture. I do love you, and yes, I want you here with me, always."

The next morning, I wake up to the sound of voices in the livingroom, just beyond the bedroom door. The smell of bacon cooking, makes me realize how hungry I am. I reach for Kevin, wanting to kiss his lips and tell him good morning, but he and Dallas are nowhere to be seen.

I lie in the bed for a few minutes, listening to the sounds of our family and friends in the livingroom. Daddy's talking to Dallas, I can hear his baby talk and then I hear Brittany, doing exactly the same. Matt and Kevin are talking to one another and then I hear Kevin's mom talking to Mr. William's. I smile, taking in all of the love and loving all of the voices now filling my house.

"Can you believe this, Darry? Our families are so wonderful, and she is so loved and cared for, babe. We love you and we miss you too. I wish you could be here to lay with me, listening to all of this... I hope you're at least watching us from up there." I whisper, talking to the air around me. The bedroom door cracks open slowly and then it opens all the way and Kevin steps through. "Mornin'. Who are you talking to?" He asks, looking around.

"I was just talking to Darry. Telling him about all of the love out there in the livingroom right now." I tell him, smiling at his sweet face.

"Oh yeah?" He says, crawling on his hands and knees up from the foot of the bed. He hovers over me and kisses my forehead, sitting back on his legs, he says, "He sees everything going on, I promise you. God's letting him see Dallas, I'm sure of it."

I love how understanding Kevin is and how he is always encouraging me, telling me that Darry sees us and that he is watching over our daughter. He's so loving and caring, he doesn't even flinch when I tell him I was thinking of Darry or talking to him, he is just immediately supportive.

I don't know what I'd do if he were ever jealous or hurt by my love for Darry. I'm so happy that I don't have to find out.

CHAPTER EIGHTEEN

When we walk out into the livingroom, all eyes are on us. "Morning sleepyhead", Matt says first. "Morning", everyone else says, greeting us as I wipe the sleep from my eyes. My daddy's holding Dallas, his arms supporting the length of her body, his hands cupped and resting under her head as she lays on his legs. Britt's sitting on the couch next to him, leaning over Dallas, making faces at her. Dallas is just looking up at them both, moving her eyes from one face to the next, a look on her face that says, "You people are nuts!" I can't help but get tickled, and giggle at her expressions.

"Who made breakfast?" I ask, looking around the room for the person to thank. "That would be Kevin", my daddy says, looking up from his granddaughter and nodding his head toward the man standing beside me. I turn to look at him over my shoulder and he grins down at me, bending down to kiss the tip of my nose. "You want to go grab some now while she's occupied?" He asks, holding his arm out as if to say, "You first".

I turn and go into the kitchen and see the delicious spread before us. The counter has plates of bacon, scrambled eggs, pancakes, toast, and all of our different flavors of jellies and jams. Kevin loves jam on everything.

"Why did you make all of this?" I ask, confused by the amount of food on the counter. "I didn't know who all would be hungry or what they'd want, so I made what I could."

I look again and ask, "Did anyone eat?" And he laughs. "No, we were waiting for you to wake up. I just finished it all, it should still be warm." He walks over to put his hand over the eggs and then the pancakes, "Yeah, it's still warm. I'll get everybody." Dallas's bedroom is closer to the kitchen than our room, so Daddy takes her and lays her down in her crib and winds her mobile for her. Everyone joins us in the kitchen and sits down around the table, filling their plates with food. It all smells so good; I feel my belly rumble and take a big bite of pancakes with blueberry jam on top. Kevin takes a mouthful of eggs and turns to smile at me, his cheeks chipmunking out, and I laugh. His mom smacks his arm and tells him to take smaller bites and to mind his manners. He turns to her and crosses his eyes, opening his mouth to show her the chewed-up food, and I laugh again as she cringes at the nasty sight.

"What are you, 12?" She asks, rolling her eyes, eating a piece of bacon. Kevin nods at her, only annoying her further. But she smiles at him and takes another bite.

Matt and Brittany tell us all that Joel is going home from the hospital today. He's been cleared and though he isn't back to one hundred percent, he's going to make a full recovery. I'm very thankful to God for sparing his life and for not taking him from us, from Jessica. Matt tells us that Joel wants to come by sometime in the next few days; he wants to meet Dallas and see how we're doing too. We didn't want to take her to the hospital because of the germs and we're a bit protective with her being so small.

Kevin lights up at the news and is nodding his head in agreement, "Yeah, dude! Tell him and Jess to come on anytime, whenever they're ready. It's not like we go anywhere." He says, laughing at his own sarcastic joke.

Mr. Williams is listening carefully to hear how Joel is recovering and I can see both joy and sadness in his eyes, and I know exactly how he's feeling. I recognize the same look I've seen in my own eyes, in the mirror, a lot over these past few months. Happiness over Joel's recovery but sad that Darry couldn't recover to be here with us now. It's a fine line there, between happiness and envy. But we're walking it.

He catches me looking at him and gives me a half smile, that I return, and he understands that I understand. He nods and takes another bite, looking down at his plate for the rest of the meal.

When I'm done eating, I go into the nursery to see Dallas. She's laying in the middle of the crib on her back, kicking her feet and moving her arms, just watching the mobile that is now silent and has stopped moving. I watch her for just a few seconds, taking her in, her eyes, her lips, the shape of her face, it's all him.

If I close my eyes and concentrate hard enough, I can hear his voice and picture him walking into the room behind me, putting his hands on my shoulders, pressing his body against my back, as we both look down to watch out beautiful baby girl, together.

I lean over the side of the crib and lift her out, putting her to my chest, I turn to walk out and see Kevin standing in the door, watching us quietly, a soft expression on his face. "She's perfect, isn't she?" He asks, kissing her cheek as we pass by him, exiting the nursery.

I smile and nod, but continue walking, ready to make it to the couch so I can love on her and try to push thoughts of Darry out of my mind. "We're gonna run, we're gonna go help Joel and Jessica get settled into his parents' house." Brittany tells us, bending down to kiss the back of Dallas's head and rubbing her back. "Love you, little girl. See you later." She whispers over her. "See y'all later too", she says, waving bye. "Later, man", Matt says to Kevin, doing that silly hand grab, chest bump, half hug thing they all do. "Yeah, later, brother. Y'all be safe."

They walk out the door and Bobby gets up to follow behind them. "Got chores to finish up, so I'm headed that way too. See y'all later." He walks out the door and I know by the slump in his shoulders that he's having a hard time of it today too.

My heart aches for him, because I completely understand.

CHAPTER NINETEEN

When everyone is gone, and the baby is down for the night, me and Kevin sit down to cuddle and watch tv. It's Saturday night, our one night that we get alone, because it's date night for everyone else. Our date is watching a new stand-up comic battle, eating popcorn for dinner and drinking cherry soda. It's not a night at the theater or swimming at the falls, but it's still nice.

Leaning against Kevin while he's watching a comedy show is like being on a waterbed with someone jumping on it. Every time he laughs, I bounce up and down. "Ugh... I'm getting seasick!" I say, teasing him. "Oh yeah? Seasick, huh?" He asks, lurching his body, teasing me back. "Mmmhmm", I nod, grinning at him, trying to egg him on, wanting to see how far I can go before he has to react in some way.

He shocks me, grabbing me suddenly by the shoulders and turning my body, laying me down on my back on the couch beside him. He straddles me and begins tracing the outline of my neck with his fingertips, moving down to my shoulders and then down my arms. His expression is dark with desire, when he reaches my hips, he grabs them with both hands, and leans in to kiss me.

I reach up and grab the back of his head, pulling him into for a deeper kiss. His fingers begin to move again, to my stomach and he's tickling me!!

"What...? Kevin!" I scream between involuntary bursts of laughter. *Yeah, I really misread his expression!*

I squirm and squeal under his touch, which only makes him continue tickling me. He's laughing too, and both of our faces are bright red.

"You... really suck, Kevin Jones!" I scream, wriggling under him, trying to break free of this torture.

"I suck? Really? Seriously? I suck, huh? Ok..." He says in a tone that tells me I'm in real trouble now. He starts to sit back on his legs, and I watch him very carefully, trying to calculate his next move. He's almost fully back so, I take my chance to make a break for it and roll myself off of the couch, freeing my body from underneath his and I take off running for the kitchen so I can get to the back door, knowing if I can just get out that door, I'll be able to lose him in the trees.

I make it to the door, laughing like crazy, but determined at the same time; he's right behind me the whole way. I can hear him breathing heavily and just as he's about to reach me, I open the door and break through into freedom. I take off like a bullet, running for the tree line. But I don't hear footsteps behind me anymore. I turn to look over my shoulder and see Kevin standing right outside the backdoor on the halfway on the porch. He's bent over, his hands on his knees as he tries to catch his breath.

I do the same and then look up at him, "What? You chicken? You going to let a girl beat you that easily?" I call back, taunting him, trying to get at his ego so he'll have to come after me.

He puts his finger up in the air, telling me to hold on, and then he stands up to say, "You win. I can't leave this porch; Dallas is sleeping inside." And he turns to go back into the house, closing the door behind him.

I stay at the wood line for a moment, skeptical that he'd give up that easily; I'm not that naive, I know he's lurking, waiting for me to come in that door so he can pounce.

So, I tiptoe out of the tree line and quietly slink around to the front porch instead. I put my foot on the first step and suddenly I'm being lifted into the air and thrown over Kevin's shoulder. "Put me down!" I scream, kicking and writhing the whole time. "Stop that before you make me drop you, girl!" He tells me, sternly.

"You're coming with me", I have something for you, he tells me, reaching up to smack my butt. He carries me into the house, through the foyer and down the hall, turning into the kitchen. The table is set up with our best dishes, wine glasses and one of my red apple cinnamon scented candles. He sits me down in a chair and tells me he's going to cook dinner for us; he says that he bought something special just for tonight.

He goes to the freezer and pulls out two steaks, then crouching down in front of the refrigerator, he reaches in and pulls out a stalk of asparagus. He moves over to the pantry, taking out two big russet potatoes, taking them over to the counter to wrap them in aluminum foil. He smiles at me and begins breaking asparagus spears. "We may not be able to go out for a nice dinner, but that doesn't mean we have to stay in and eat canned pasta. So, you just sit there, and enjoy the view." He says, turning his backside to me, poking it out and peeking back over his shoulder at me with a big grin on his face.

"That's quite the view there", I tell him, smiling because it's not untrue. He looks amazing in his jeans and his tight black t-shirt. He's normally dressed in button downs and dark jeans or khakis, but tonight he's dressed down for staying in and relaxing.

He seasons the steaks while he's heating up the grill that's sitting on the counter, and while he's waiting, he tosses the aluminum foil wrapped potatoes into the oven. The asparagus is already in the frying pan on the stove. He cuts a lemon in half and I know it's for me. I love lemon juice on everything. He squeezes it over the asparagus and my steak. I smile at how well he seems to know me. He smiles back and continues working.

He was playing around telling me to enjoy the view, but I really am. He moves so gracefully around the kitchen. I guess he's a true artist in everything he does, not just in those sketchbooks he's always carrying around. Watching him cook is like watching a professional cooking show; now he's chopping onions and mushrooms to top the steaks with, and he looks like he's had professional culinary training, the way he chops them so quickly and smoothly. He turns his face up at me, still chopping, and smiles, "I cooked a lot at my parents' house", he tells me, reading my thoughts, and winking at me.

He picks up the knife and slides the onions off with his finger, then he picks the mushrooms up with the same blade and tosses it all together in a small frying pan over melted butter. He seasons the vegetables and puts the steaks on the now hot grill. Then, with everything cooking, he walks over to me and kisses me; he's got lemon juice on his lips. I didn't even see him do it. He looks at me, still kissing me and smiles, making me kiss his teeth.

"You're so silly", I tell him, playfully smacking his chest and kissing him again.

"This kitchen smells incredible!" I tell him when all the delicious aromas begin to mesh together, filling my nostrils and making my stomach grumble hungrily.

He goes to turn off the asparagus, removing it from the heat of the stove. "You know, there's nothing sexier than a man who can cook", I tell him, half teasing, half completely serious. He is so sexy moving around this kitchen right now, chopping, tossing, flipping, tasting, watching how his muscles flex and move with each different movement, the smile on his face and then the look of concentration. He's pretty hot right now.

When everything is done, he makes my plate and brings it to the table, sitting it in front of me. Then he makes his plate, bringing it to sit directly across from me. Right before I pick up my first bite, he takes half of a lemon and squeezes the juice over everything on my plate, looking me in my eyes with a sexy half grin on his face. He sits back in his chair, still licking the juice from his fingers. "Thank you", I tell him, completely in awe of all he's just done, including knowing to put lemon on everything on my plate, including the potato.

We eat in silence, which would be awkward normally, but somehow this just feels different. The way he watches me so intently as I eat and how he's taking his bites so slowly, lingering as if to savor each and every morsel, it feels like the sexiest meal I've ever sat through. He smiles at me from time to time, giving me this look, his beautiful green eyes pull at me as he's giving me his best sultry stare, making it difficult for me to finish my meal.

When he's had his fill, he removes his plate and glass, and comes back for mine. I stopped eating a few minutes ago, unable to take my eyes off of him, unable to think straight; my mind full of images that I have no right to have in my head.

He walks over to me, standing right in front of me. I have to look up at him as he stands over me, and he leans down, putting his hands on my back and running them up my neck, and around to my cheeks, lifting my face toward him, he bends down to kiss me. "I love you, Alley", he whispers to me. "I love you too, Kevin."

CHAPTER TWENTY

As the weeks turn into months, and the seasons are changing around us, we see Dallas beginning to smile and laugh, clinging to Kevin more and more. She's definitely a daddy's girl. He's so great with her, loving her as if she had come from him. And of course, she doesn't know that she didn't, she just loves him because of how he loves her, how he's been there for her, and how he will always be there for her. She has him wrapped around her little finger too; she knows, he knows it, we all know it.

We see her begin to hold her head up by herself and then she's rolling over from her back to her stomach. This is where things start to get tricky. We can't leave her on the couch while we run to the other room anymore. And forget making her stay on her side to sleep. She's going to sleep in her belly now, like it or not. It doesn't matter how many times Kevin wakes up, turning her back to her side, she turns right back to her belly.

She's stubborn. She knows what she wants, and you best bet she's going to get it. I don't know where she could've gotten that.

She's not a fussy girl though. She's very laid back, actually. She watches us all; everyone around her. Brittany's always messing with her, moving from side to side around the room, seeing if she will follow her with her eyes, and she does. She smiles, a lot and she seems to be easily entertained. She will lay and play with toys on her own on the floor, lying on her little blanket for the longest time, which makes it easy to get household chores done.

Kevin likes to play 'funny faces' with her. He will make a face and then laugh his head off watching her try to mimic it.

She really loves Matt and Joel too, who have definitely stepped up into the role of Uncle Matt and Uncle Joel. Jessica loves her, but she doesn't want to admit it. She likes to act like she just tolerates her, but I can see how she really feels when she thinks no one's looking and she smiles at her or whispers baby talk to her, looking around to see if anyone's listening. She adores her but she has to keep up the tough girl facade for some reason.

Her Uncle Joel absolutely loves her and is tickled by her every time he's with her. "Man, she is so smart!" He's always telling us. "Look at how she copies me!" He'll say, laughing as she waves back to him or sticks her tongue out at him, laughing with him as she does it. He'll make his eyes go big and wide and she'll do the same and then fall back laughing. It's the cutest thing to watch; the two of them playing together. It's so sweet how much they love each other.

Now Uncle Matt, he's here each and every weekend, sitting with her watching the guys old recorded football games on Saturdays and Sundays. He says he's conditioning her, getting her ready for real games and he's convinced that he's going to make her love the game so much she'll want to play in high school. He's a nut.

She's only four months old, but he doesn't care. He says you can't start them too early.

Brittany spoils her with cute clothes and shoes. She brings her a new outfit every week just about. Oh, and accessories too. She's got tights with polka dots and some with ruffly butts. She's got the cutest little plastic necklaces and so many barrettes, hair bows and hair bands that she had to have a little drawer designated just for holding them all.

All of her grandparents are absolutely head over heels for her. Between my parents, Darry's parents and Kevin's parents, we're lucky to see her at all. They're all the time coming by to pick her up and take her shopping or just back to their house to play for a few hours and sometimes they'll keep her overnight, which is a great help to us, allowing us some much-needed alone time to just rest or watch a movie together that doesn't have talking animals or colorful underwater worlds..

Beth loves her, and she's actually here quite a bit, just hanging out on the floor with her. She will put the phone down for most of the visit too. Robby comes over to see her from time to time, but he's a 13-year-old boy, he's not really too interested in babies. I think a lot of the time that he is here, it's because Beth is.

It's been great having all of the help and the love pouring in over her and on us too. She knows she's loved, that's for sure. And because of all of that love and attention, she's the happiest baby I've ever seen.

Today, Kevin and my daddy have planned an outing for all of us. It's March, so the weather has been a little chilly for going outside still, but it's getting nicer. Kevin, being the amazing man that he is, has noticed that I've had cabin fever and has planned an outdoor picnic for all of us.

We're not leaving the farm, but we'll be outside for a little bit. He's got some kites and I'm almost positive that Matt will bring a football. My mom is bringing the sandwiches, Elaine's bringing the chips, we'll have drinks and cups and plates, and Kevin's mom is bringing the potato salad, which is great because I love her potato salad.

"Hey, babe", whatcha doin?" Kev walks into the nursery, where I'm pulling Dallas's clothes out for the picnic. It's still a little chilly and the wind has been picking up, so I know she'll need to be bundled up pretty well. "Just getting Dally's clothes ready for this afternoon", I tell him. "Ok, well I'm gonna run to my mom's house real quick to pick her up, dad's not feeling well today, so he won't be here", he kisses my cheek, leaving the room. I grab her a pair of her leggings that Britt bought for her, they're black with tiny little pink hearts all over them, and a memory comes back to me of walking into the kitchen and seeing Kevin in my apron, cooking at the stove with tiny little pink hearts all over him. I can't help but laugh at the memory.

I get Dally dressed and take her to the livingroom, lying her down on her blanket with her plushies.

I go fix a cup of coffee and grab some strawberries from the refrigerator. Sitting at the table, thumbing through one of Kev's sketchbooks that he left in the kitchen, I hear him pulling up the driveway. Before he can make it to the door, I have Dallas in my arms, and we're headed outside to greet them both. I look out into the yard and see faces of the people I love most in my life putting down blankets on the grass and sitting down baskets and bags of food. Kevin is helping his mom out of his truck, when he looks back at me and winks.

He comes over to us and kisses the top of Dallas's bonnet that's tied firmly around her head and then he kisses me and pulls me into a hug. "You ready?" He asks, taking my hand and walking me over to the crowd.

Elaine takes Dallas from me right away and lays her in the middle of the blanket, where all of the grandparents instantly come to gather around her. Mary, Kevin's mom, is smiling and making baby noises at her, tickling her little belly. Dally's eating it up, cooing and trying to talk to everyone. Mary hands her a stuffed animal and she gnaws on its ear.

Matt grabs a kite and starts trying to get it in the air. Kevin's right behind him, trying to race him with his own kite.

Daddy, Robby and Bobby are all behind us, throwing Matt's football around, everyone is happy and playing, just having a great time together. It's the best day I've had in a long time.

I sit and watch them all, talking with all of the ladies surrounding me when Kevin gives up on his kite and comes to sit with me. Matt's kite is doing really well, it's above the trees, flying with great confidence.

Kevin gets my attention by grabbing my elbow and turning me toward him. "Hey, can I ask you something before we eat?" He asks me, a small grin on his face. I look at him and back to Dallas and then to all of the faces now looking at the both of us, surprisingly not full of curiosity.

Kevin stands up, pulling me with him. He kisses my cheek and begins to bend down in front of me. He's looking up at my eyes the whole time, wanting to hold my focus on him, not wanting it to move to anyone else.

"Alley, I told you when I gave you that ring", he says, nodding toward the silver diamond band on my right hand, "that I would ask you to marry me one day. Alley, I love you more than I have ever loved anyone. You are everything to me, all I need in this life. Well, you and Dally", he smiles at our daughter and looks back up at me, as the tears begin to fall to my cheeks. "I don't ever want to be away from either of you as long as I have a choice. Please, say you'll marry me, Alley, and let me take care of the both of you, for the rest of our lives." He's looking at me, his eyes full of hope and love.

I pull him up to me and throw my arms around him. I kiss him and then I tell him, "Yes, I'll marry you, Kevin!"

Everyone is clapping and when I look at their faces, they're crying with me.

CHAPTER TWENTY-ONE

The rest of the picnic is spent ohhhing and awwing over the beautiful ring he had just proposed with. It had been his grandmother's wedding ring; she gave it to his mom to hold for him, so he could give it to his future wife. It's so beautiful; the band is gold, and instead of the traditional diamond setting, there's a big white pearl set in the center. Around the pearl are tiny little diamonds coming out of both sides in the shape of triangles.

At first neither of us knew what to do with the ring since I was still wearing Darry's ring. Elaine had to come tell us that I was supposed to move Darry's ring to my right finger, where Kevin's promise ring now was. So, I move Darry's ring to my right hand and let Kevin slip his ring on my wedding finger. I put the promise ring inside in my jewelry box for now, until I can get it sized and can slip it on my finger next to Darry's ring.

The picnic went well, everyone congratulated us and the mom's spent the remainder of the lunch whispering about wedding details, while the dads talked business stuff. They all took turns swooning over Dally, until it was her nap time, and Kevin picked her up to take her inside to lay her down.

I was happy to have a moment of separation between us, it gave me time to process what all had just happened, without him here to study each and every expression that might come across my face as I sat in deep thought.

Not that I have to think about wanting to marry Kevin, I do want to marry him. I love him, so very much. He's great to us, to Dallas. He's the best daddy to her and we already live as if we're married. Heck, it feels kind of like when Darry died, Kevin just kind of slipped in and took over his role. That's a horrible thought. I don't really feel like he took over Darry's role, but he took care of me after Darry died, and then he took care of us, when Dally was born. He's been here every moment since.

The thing that keeps running through my mind is, I'm still married. I know it's legally not true, I'm widowed. But in my heart, in my head, I'm still married. Next month, I'll be 19 years old, and I will have been married, widowed and remarried before I'm 20. It just seems a bit much, a bit fast.

I hear the front door open and close and snap back to the conversations happening around me. Joel and Matt are talking cars and football; the usual for those two. While Britt and Jess are talking bridesmaids and reception details. "Are you going to wear white again?" Jess asks and Brittany gives her a scornful look. "I-I don't know. I haven't really thought about it", I tell her, looking from her to Britt and then to my mom. I don't even realize I'm crying until my mom gets up and comes to put her arm around me.

"What is it, Alley?" she leans in and whispers to me, trying not to bring too much attention to us and our current situation.

I shrug my shoulders, unable to speak and she hugs me tighter.

Kevin makes it to the blanket and kneels beside me and my mom. She looks up at him and backs up as he slides in to take her place. "Hey, you, let's go talk somewhere real fast, ok?" And he lifts me up by my hands, leading me back to our front porch where we sit on the steps.

"What's going on, Alley? Why are you upset?" he asks, fear and uncertainty filling up his voice.

I shrug my shoulders, not wanting to let too much of what's going on in my head, slip out and fall all over him.

"You have to talk to me here, babe. I can't help if you won't tell me what's wrong." he pleads.

The look in his eyes breaks my heart, making me want to tell him everything I've been thinking, but the logical side of me knows it's better not to tell him because it'll only hurt him more. But before I can say a word, he says, "Are you having doubts about accepting my proposal, Alley? Is that what I saw on your face before I came out the door a few minutes ago?" A sadness appears in his eyes as he already knows the answer. I just nod and he nods back, "I thought that might be it."

We sit in silence for a few minutes and then he says, "Alley, let me ask you something, please." I look up at him, and he looks back at me. "Do you love me? I mean all these months together, you, me and Dally, we've been a family. I've been there with you every step of the way. But was that because you love me? Or was it because you needed me?" I can literally hear his heart breaking as he's trying to get the words out of his mouth.

"I do love you, Kevin. I honestly do. It's just..." I stop and look down at my feet playing in the dirt below the step. "It's just that..." I look up at him, and he says, "What, Alley? It's just what?" he demands, a little more aggressively than I expected, and it throws me off. I've never really seen him upset or angry, ever. I hadn't realized just how calm he had always been until right now, when he's not so much. "Dang it, Alley! I know you loved Darry. I know I can't take his place and you won't ever be able to love me like you loved him." He's pacing in front of me now.

"Love", I say, barely loud enough for me to hear. "What was that?" he asks, leaning in so he can hear me. "Love", I say louder so he can hear, feeling a defiance rising up in me, but I don't know where it's coming from, he hasn't done anything wrong here.

"It's not past tense, Kevin! I still love him. I always will. I can't help it. He hasn't even been gone for a whole year!" The words are bursting from me before I can stop them. "I spent 18 years with him! I can't just turn it off... for you or for anyone!" I'm screaming now, still not sure why.

"Alice! I've never asked you to stop loving Darry. I've only asked that you try to make room for me in there too!" He yells back, pointing at my heart. "I am not the enemy here, Alley." He says in a softer, more loving tone. "Why are you doing this?" The tears are filling his eyes as he realizes that I'm picking a fight so I can blame him and have an excuse to make him leave.

I sit back down and look at the ground, not willing to say another word to him. "Ok, I think I understand. I get it. There's still no room for anyone but him. And there never will be." His face is flushed, his heart broken into tiny little pieces.

"Alright, Alice. I will not burden you any longer. I apologize for overstaying my welcome." He goes in the front door and grabs his keys, "I'll have Matt or Joel get my stuff another time. I don't want anyone to disturb Dallas right now." He walks down the steps to his truck and opens the door to get in. He turns to take one last look at me before he gets in to leave, his eyes red and swollen from crying. He looks at me with such despair but then something unexpected happens, his expression changes into one of anger and he's looking at me like he doesn't know me... and like he wouldn't want to. He gets in and slams his door, turning the truck around, he goes to the side of my parent's house and tells Mary to come on, they're leaving. She gets in and he takes off down the driveway, tearing into the gravel and throwing dust everywhere.

When his truck is no longer in sight, I break down, my chest heaving up and down as the tears won't stop falling. My mom, Britt and Elaine are all by my side in seconds. "It's ok. It's ok." My mom says to me, smoothing my hair and pulling me to her. "What happened?" Brittany asks, in a hushed whisper. I try my best to tell them through the sobs, "I-I-I don't know!" I manage to cry out.

Dallas starts crying and my daddy goes in to take care of her.

Elaine is sitting next to me and she asks in a very quiet, loving tone, "Sweetheart, are you confused and feeling guilty about accepting Kevin's proposal because of Darry?" I look up at her through my bloodshot eyes and nod. Putting my hands over my face, I cry and cry.

"Oh, baby. You don't have to feel guilty. You and Kevin, you two share a beautiful bond, Darry would be so happy that you two have each other. He wouldn't want you to spend years wasted away on his memory. He would never be ok with you missing out on love because of him. Of course, he would want to be the one here with you, Alice, but since he can't be, I know with all my heart that my son would be overjoyed that it was someone he loved and trusted, that would be sharing your life with you and raising his daughter."

I stop sobbing and wipe my nose with the back of my sleeve. "That's kind of gross", Jess says as she approaches us. I smile at her honesty and she leans in to tell me, "Get yourself together, girl. Darry loved you. He never shut up about you and how he wanted your life to be great. He would want you to marry Kevin in his absence, duh." I don't know what to say, I just laugh and laugh and laugh some more. "Man, you are seriously bi-polar or something", she says, and then she smiles at me and gives me a hug.

"Seriously though, don't hold yourself back in Darry's name. It's not him making you feel this way, it's your own doubts and fears. Do you love Kevin?" she asks me, looking me right in the eye. "Yes, very much", I tell her, "But he's gone for good now, I'm sure of it."

"I wouldn't be so sure if I were you. Darry's not the only one that's been brooding over you since we were kids. That kind of obsessive love doesn't just go away with one stupid fight, Alley." Matt says as he walks over to us, sitting down and putting his arm around Brittany. "I should know", he says as he snuggles her neck.

"He'll be back", Joel adds, coming to put his arm around Jessica. "He loves you just like Darry did. He was just smart enough not to speak up about it around Darry... or you. But me and Matt, we got to listen to it constantly. From the third grade, til now. He won't be able to stay away from you, or from his daughter." He adds, reminding me that this isn't just about me or Kevin, she loves him too. And he loves her.

I nod and wipe my eyes. "Ok. I'll give him some time to calm down and then I'll try calling him. I love you guys! You're honestly the best family I could have ever asked for."

CHAPTER TWENTY-TWO

A few days go by and the house feels so empty around me. It's just me and Dallas, with the occasional visit from Mom or Daddy, Darry's parents or one of the group, but it's mostly been me and Dally here, hanging out, spending time together.

I have to get out of the house today. These walls feel like they're closing in on me. I cannot watch another cartoon or talk show. My mind is full of thoughts and doubts, but mostly, I just miss him.

I get Dally dressed and carry her outside. We're going to the barn this morning to see who all is hanging out there. I know that Kevin's been helping my dad out, and I'm secretly hoping he'll be there now. He really needs to get back to school; I'm going to be graduating late, but he could still catch up. However, today is Sunday, so it's very likely that he could be in there with them, helping with random chores.

When we reach the barn, we hear people talking and laughing together. I see that Daddy is talking to Bobby, they're standing by the office door, leaned slightly in, looking inside and then back to each other during conversation.

"Good morning", I say as me and Dally come around the door. "What's going on in here today?" Daddy looks up at us, smiling and Bobby comes over to talk sweetly to his granddaughter, reaching out to pick her up.

He walks her into the office, where I'm guessing Mom and Elaine are. Daddy gives me a hug and asks me how I'm doing. "I'm ok, just getting cabin fever, I suppose." He nods, understanding exactly what I mean and puts his arm around my shoulders, bringing me to the office door where Bobby and he were just standing.

I look in the office and sure enough, there's Mom, sitting behind her desk, a stack of papers in front of her that she's trying to concentrate on in between conversation. Elaine's sitting in the chair across from her, also working on a pile of paperwork. "That's the good thing about running your own business, you can take work anywhere you see fit", Elaine says looking at me out of the corner of her eye, still crunching numbers and writing and then scratching things out.

"How's the new one doing?" I ask, remembering the foal that was born not long ago. "Doing good, getting bigger by the day", Daddy tells me.

"Has Kev been by? I only ask because I know he was helping out while he was here", I ask, as I look down at my feet, hoping they don't detect the desperation in my voice.

"Naw, he's keeping his distance, I believe. That boy doesn't know his head from his butt right now. He's probably just trying to figure things out. He won't be around here... not any time soon anyway", Bobby tells me, and I feel the punch right in my gut from the truth and honesty in his words.

"Yeah, I guess not", I say, turning to leave the barn.

Not wanting to go home, but wanting to give him his space and time to calm down, I put Dallas in the car and buckle her in. "We're gonna go to church today, baby girl." I tell her, kissing her forehead and climbing into the front seat.

I pull out of the driveway and turn toward town, anxious to get as far away from this place as possible.

In town, people are piling into the church; some lingering on the front steps in deep conversation, while others stand in the foyer, greeting each other as they pass through to the sanctuary.

I park the car and get Dallas out of the backseat. Unsure of the decision I've made to come here, I stand back in hesitation, not knowing what to expect. It's been a long time since I've been through those doors, but it hasn't been long enough that I wouldn't expect to be bombarded with sympathies and pity over Darry's death.

Not wanting to return to the farm to sit alone in my own thoughts, feeling lonely and depressed, I walk forward, gaining more confidence in my choice to come to church today with every step.

If they give their condolences – again, I will just nod and shake their outstretched hand or return their well-intentioned hug. I think to myself, stepping up onto the first step into the building.

Pastor Rainey is the first to greet me, doing exactly what I expected, well.... kind of. "Well, well, well... look who we have here", he says, putting his hand on his hip, exaggerating his astonishment at my being here. "To what do we owe this lovely surprise?" he asks, taking Dally's hand in his, shaking it gently, as if to introduce himself. "Hi, there, beautiful girl. I'm happy to see your bright, cheery face here this morning", he tells her leaning into her face as he speaks, a big joyful smile on his face.

I can't help but smile at his jovial demeanor, and the seemingly ecstatic reaction to our being here. "I haven't seen you since Darry's passing, I just want to tell you how sorry we all are and tell you that we have not stopped praying for you and little Dallas here", he continues, tickling her chunky little leg, making her laugh. "I hope this will be the first of many return visits", he says to me, smiling, as I thank him for his kind words and start into the church.

When we get inside of the Sanctuary, I see the pews are beginning to fill up, so I hurry to find a seat in the fourth row on the right side of the room. Once we're seated, I place Dallas on my lap and begin to look around the room, taking in the faces of all those surrounding us. I've tried to stay close to home lately, not really venturing out too much more than is absolutely necessary, so I haven't seen most of these people much recently.

I continue to look around until I lock eyes with someone staring intently in our direction. The beautiful green eyes now holding my attention, both startle and excite me. Kevin's here too, sitting across from us on the left side of the room, with his mom and dad.

CHAPTER TWENTY-THREE

The pain in Kevin's eyes when he sees us stabs me right in the chest. I want to go to him, to tell him how sorry I am and how wrong I was for behaving so harshly toward him. I want to tell him that it was all me, that none of it was his fault. But now is not a good time, service is about to begin and we're in a room full of people that do not need to know any of the details of our relationship.

All I can do is wait and pray that he understands why I haven't called him.

I sit through Pastor Rainey's sermon, doing my very best to listen and focus on the message God has laid on his heart to deliver to us today, but my mind keeps going back to Kevin, and I find myself looking in his direction. He looks as if he may be having a hard time too as he shifts in his seat, over and over again, his eyes on Pastor Rainey but the distracted expression on his face says he's not focused on the sermon either.

When he gets up and walks to the back of the church, disappearing through the doors behind us, I wait a few minutes and follow him out front.

He's pacing on the front lawn, his hands on his hips, his head down as he stares at the ground in front of him with each step. He doesn't even look up when he says, "Why did you come here today? You don't go to church. Did you come just to torment me?"

His words have frozen my feet to the spot where I stand. I'm caught off guard by his assumption, not knowing what to say, feeling both hurt by his words and shocked that he would believe such a thing.

"What? No, Kevin. Why would you even say that?" I ask, trying to hide the disappointment in my voice. "I didn't even know you'd be here."

He finally stops pacing and looks at us, his expression dark, full of anguish, and maybe a little angry too. But when he sees Dally, his expression lightens. He doesn't say a word, he crosses the distance between us and scoops her into his arms, kissing her cheek. He steps back a few steps and asks, "How's she doing?"

"She's doing fine. I think she misses you though. She's cried a little more at night, I think she's missing y'all's time together." *I miss you too, terribly. I wish you'd forgive me and come home.* I want to say it out loud, I want to tell him, but I can see how tense he already is, and I don't want to have an argument in front of the church right before it lets out.

That's all I need, for the congregation to see us having it out on church grounds, the first time I've visited in forever. They'd think I came today just to fight with him. No, thank you. I'm sure everyone will already think badly of me when they find out me and Kevin are together, if they don't already know; word does travel quickly in this small town.

"I miss her too", he admits, hugging her close to him and kissing the top of her head. "I don't like being away from her."

"Kevin, can you come home so we can talk please?" I ask, hoping he will agree, and we can work this out.

He hands her back to me, saying, "I don't think that's a good idea, Alley. I don't think either one of us is ready for that."

He turns and walks away, getting into his truck, he cranks it up and backs out of the parking spot. He squeals tires out of the church parking lot, and takes off through town, driving towards his parent's house.

I don't know what to think as I stand here, unable to move, contemplating the scene he just made trying to get himself as far from me as possible, as quickly as he could. He is either very angry, very hurt, or a lot of both. And I can't blame him, but I can't help how I feel either, well how I felt. Darry was everything to me, he's the father of my child, the love of my life, my best friend, and now my angel watching over us. The feelings of guilt that come from me feeling as if I am somehow betraying him and his memory, our marriage, the love we had for each other, I can't just turn that off. I wish Kevin could understand that.

But in all honesty, I know that Kevin isn't angry or hurt over my feelings for Darry, and I know he would understand my feelings about betraying Darry, if I had given him the chance to. I didn't try to explain anything to him, I had just lashed out at him for no good reason. I know why he's upset. I had agreed to marry him and then I had freaked out on him. And in front of everyone we love, no less. I had hurt and humiliated him all at the same time. I am the worst kind of person.

I walk over to the car and put Dally into her car seat and then I get in the front seat, putting the key in, but not turning it. I rest my forehead on the steering wheel, trying to wrap my head around our confrontation, if that's what you could even call it. I feel horrible, and I want to tell him. I want him to listen to me. But I understand that he doesn't want to get dragged back into this chaos, this indecisiveness. He is done with the ups and downs, just like I knew he would be one day.

As people begin to come out of the front doors, I turn the key and leave the parking lot. I head through town, passing all the same stores, all the same people and places that Kevin just passed. I'm picking up speed and before I know it, I'm pulling into his parent's driveway.

When I pull up to the house, Kevin comes out of the front door, letting the screen door slam shut behind him. His parent's house is a cute little white farmhouse with a wraparound porch. They have old white rocking chairs sitting on the porch, lining the wall all the way down the front. I love their house; it has a lot of history and a ton of charm. His great-great grandfather had been forced to build the house when their original home on the property was struck by lightning, burning it to the ground in the middle of the night, leaving them homeless with 5 young kids. It's an amazing story, one that I love to hear Kevin tell.

His great-great grandparents had lived in a small shed with all of their children, while his great-great grandfather and their surrounding neighbors labored over this house, day and night, trying to get it ready by winter, which was fast approaching. The shed had just enough space for all of them to sleep on blankets that they spread out on the floor each night. The kids would draw water from the well, and they'd all take turns "bathing" out of a pail. They'd eat meals outside on a picnic table their daddy had thrown together with old barn wood from years ago, when they had needed to expand their barn space.

They used the bathroom by digging holes in the ground and then filling them back in when they were done.

It's incredible how resilient they were and how they had refused to allow anyone to take them in, not wanting to be a burden on their family or neighbors.

Kevin's looking at me, wondering why I'm here, when he just told me he didn't want to talk. I grab Dallas out of the car and walk toward him. He stays on the front porch, leaning against the post at the top of the stairs. "What are you doing here, Alley?" He asks, his tone full of confusion and warning.

"I need to talk to you, Kevin", I tell him, stepping forward, bringing Dallas with me. "We need to talk about this."

"Alley, I think you've said all you need to say, don't you? You aren't ready for us; you're still married to Darry. And

I understand that it's hard for you to let him go, I really do. But I don't think I can stay there with the two of you anymore", he says, his tone very guarded. "I can't keep loving you like I do, knowing it's only a matter of time and you will make me leave because I'm not him. I'll never be Darry, Alice."

CHAPTER TWENTY-FOUR

His words cut right through me and I know just how badly I've hurt him. "Kevin, I don't want you to be Darry. You're right, you and no one else can replace him. We spent our lives together. But I love you too Kevin, and I don't want to replace Darry with you. I want to be with you, because you make me happy and I don't want to be without you. I want to marry you, Kevin. I was wrong before, I just got overwhelmed and felt guilty, like I was forgetting Darry or something." I look down, not wanting him to see the pain in my face at the thought of forgetting my husband.

He walks toward me, his guard down, and he puts his arms around me and Dally. "Alice, I understand, and I don't want you to forget him. I won't forget him either, and I want Dally to know all about him too. I don't think we're betraying him or his memory by loving each other, and I'm sorry that you felt that way and that you were dealing with it alone." He kisses me, and Dally squeals, tugging at his shirt.

"So, does this mean you'll come home?" I ask, feeling brave suddenly. He smiles and nods, "Yeah, I'll come home."

He takes Dally and says, "She's riding with me though." They walk over to his truck and he puts her in her car seat in his backseat. He leans in and whispers to her, "I've missed you little girl." And kisses her cheek before closing the door.

"I'll race you there! We have a wedding to plan!" He says excitedly, stepping up into his truck and closing the door.

"I don't think so, Kevin Jones! You better drive carefully. You have and are precious cargo!" I yell at him, getting into my car.

He leads the way to our house, being sure to drive extra carefully; to the point that I begin to think he's being sarcastic.

When we get to our house, my parents are sitting on their front porch with Darry's parents. Daddy gives me a thumbs up and Elaine nods her approval as we pass by them. My heart flutters at their acceptance and constant support. I don't know where I'd be without all of them. I'd probably be a crazy mess, even more than I am now.

Kevin gets Dallas out of the truck and walks over to me. Holding her on his hip, he bends down to look me in the eyes, telling me, "Let's make sure this is the last time we're ever apart, ok? I was losing my mind being away from the two of you", he confesses, leaning in to kiss me.

I smile at his honesty and kiss him back. "I promise. And I understand, I was going a little mad myself", I confess too, hoping he understands that it wasn't easy for me to be away from him either.

He puts his hand on my back and leads me to the house, closing the door behind us.

CHAPTER TWENTY-FIVE

"I don't think I want another big wedding, though, Mom. I don't want to wear white again either, it doesn't feel right", I tell her, for what seems like the millionth time. Me, Mom, Elaine and Dally are all sitting at her kitchen table, eating breakfast, discussing wedding details, which already feels odd considering that it wasn't that long ago that I was sitting here discussing my wedding to Darry. We've decided to wait until we have both graduated at least. We've both gone back to school, which is only possible due to both Mom and Elaine. They have taken on babysitting duties, exchanging days, in order to see us finish school. Thank fully there's only a few more months left of our senior year, it took forever for us to catch up on our missed assignments, and we had to agree to Saturday classes for the first couple of weeks to make up the missing credits.

We were both determined to walk with our friends, though, so Saturdays didn't seem like that big of a deal. Mary stepped up immediately and took Saturday's with Dally, so that made the decision easier. I think all of them were just very eager to get us through to the end of school.

Being back to school was odd at first. Everyone knew me and Darry had been married, which made it tough to walk back into school on the arm of one of his very best friends. Jessica and Joel were in Saturday classes with us for a while too, they both had some catching up to do as well after the accident and him being in a coma for so long, her staying with him.

"Alley?" I hear Mom calling me and come back to the conversation. "Yeah?" I ask, giving Dally her bottle.

"I asked if you had thought about where you want to have the wedding? When I asked you last week you said you were looking into it. So? Did you find somewhere?" She asks, slightly annoyed that I wasn't paying attention.

"Mom, I really just don't know. I thought about the park, but I don't know when we're getting married exactly, so I don't know if that's going to work. We've talked about a winter wedding, like around Christmas time, but Kevin thinks waiting until Christmas is too long", I say with an over exaggerated sigh. "I just don't know."

"Alley, no one is trying to rush you, but we do need to at least set a date so we can know when and what to plan first."

I finish feeding Dallas her bottle and clean up her messy little face. She reminds me of a baby doll, she's so cute. She smiles at me as she tries to take the washcloth from me. "Uh uh, little girl, this isn't for you", I tell her, leaning into to rub my nose to hers.

She laughs and throws her head back, being overly dramatic and expressive just like her mommy. I can't help but laugh with her. And then mom joins in on the laughter with us.

Kevin comes into the kitchen with Daddy and Robby, talking tractors and planting schedules. I don't know why but Kevin is trying to talk Daddy into using the field in the back, between our houses, to plant pumpkins and

Christmas trees. He has it in his head that we, as in he and I, could start a seasonal farm, selling only at Halloween and Christmas, and we'd somehow be set financially throughout the year. Daddy and Bobby have been very patient and actually pretty supportive of his idea, believing it to be a sound business decision. I don't get it, but hey, whatever these guys want to do, that's on them.

I'll plant some pumpkins and Christmas trees. I don't mind; then mine will all be free, and I'll have the pick of the bunch! It could work.

"Are you guys hungry?" Mom asks them, pointing to the food on the counter and stove. "Famished!" Kevin says, grabbing a piece of sausage and taking a big bite before he comes to kiss his little girl and me.

"Kevin, please tell my daughter that you guys need to set a date for the wedding." Mom tries to bring him over to the dark side, but he resists and throws it back to me. "Oh no, sorry, Mrs. Wilson, but that's all her." He sits down at the table and starts playing peek-a-boo with Dally, picking her up and taking her from me.

I stand up and walk over to the counter, putting distance and the counter between me and all of them.

"Ok, so now that everyone's here, I'm going to tell you why we haven't set a date." I look to Kevin, who encourages me to go on with a wink and a smile.

"I have thought about this and thought about this. I cannot move forward as long as I'm looking back. I have to say goodbye to Darry before I can say "I do" to Kevin." I continue talking to the very confused faces in front of me.

"Honey, I don't think I understand exactly", Bobby says, questioning what I mean.

"Well, I've decided that I'm taking my part of his remains and I'm having a small portion put into a special trinket for Dally. The rest I'll be flying out to Oceanside, where we honeymooned. I'll be releasing his ashes into the ocean where we drove along the coast our last day there, and that's where I'll say my goodbyes to him, so I can let him go and start my new life."

They're all looking around at each other, and I'm terrified that they're going to protest or be angry or upset, but they're not. They smile back at me and tell me this sounds like a solid plan, a great idea. All of them agree that I need to let him go, I need to move on, for my sake and Dally's, and Kevin's too.

"I leave a week after graduation", I inform them and go back to sit next to Kevin, who leans in, whispering, "I'm proud of you, Alley. You handled that very well."

"Well, speaking of graduation, dear", Daddy starts. "It's not very far off from now, are we having a party here after or are we babysitting while you guys go to other parties?"

We hadn't even discussed parties really. We're just glad to be graduating. I look at Kevin, who is also looking at me and we both say at the same time, "Other parties, babysitting", and laugh at both of our eagerness to get off of this farm for a while.

Everyone else is laughing with us, understanding just how badly we need to get away.

"Alrighty then", Daddy says, clapping his hands together. "I think we can plan a night with this little one, don't y'all?" He says, looking at Mom, Elaine and Bobby, reaching down to take her from Kev.

"Certainly", Bobby says, leaning in to kiss her tiny cheek.

"Hey, where are Robby and Beth?" I ask, realizing they didn't come in for breakfast.

"I don't know, they were with us in the barn", Kev tells me, looking back down the hallway, to see if they're in the livingroom.

"I'm gonna go get them, will you keep an eye on her?" I ask, pointing to Dally, who doesn't need anymore eyes on her, honestly.

I leave the house and walk out to the barn. I go through the already open doors and tiptoe through as quietly as possible, trying to sneak up and scare them. I hear them moving around, the hay making noise under their feet, and their giggles coming from the far stall on the right.

I sneak up, and jump up, looking into the stall, but I am not prepared for what I see. Robby and Beth are in the corner, making out! My little brother is kissing Darry's little sister like he's grown! "Robby Wilson!" I yell at him, "Get your butt out of there right now!" I stand firm, pointing to the barn door, "Get outside right now, both of you!"

They're both wide eyed, knowing they've been outed and they can't argue, manipulate or talk their way out of what I just saw with my own eyes.

CHAPTER TWENTY-SIX

"Calm down, Alley, geez." Robby says, rolling his eyes at me. "We weren't doing anything." He tries to convince me, not knowing exactly what I saw and just hoping that I'll buy it.

"Robby Wilson, don't you dare stand here and try to lie to my face. You had your tongue in her mouth, I saw you both with my own eyes!" I say, pointing to my wide-open eyes.

He looks down at the ground, a smug grin on his face, and turns his head halfway to peek out of the corner of his eye at Beth, who is looking down also, moving the dirt at her feet with her shoe. She turns her head slightly to peek at Robby too, and I've seen enough.

"Oh… my. Oh, no no no. You're 13!" I say to Robby, "and she's only 12!"

"She'll be 13 in two months!" He protests, trying to make this sound better.

"And you'll be 14 in three months, Robby! But that's beside the point. You're both too young for this. It's wrong."

"Why is it wrong?" He asks, stepping toward her. I stand between them and he steps back, continuing in his fight for his rights to kiss Darry's sister. "I love her, Alley! I'm going to marry her one day, just like Darry married you." He says, very matter of fact, total confidence in what he's telling me. I'm taken back for a moment, opening my mouth to speak but no words will come out.

I look from my little brother to Darry's little sister, and for the first time, I see us. I see us when we were their age, not sneaking around kissing in barn stalls, but our love for one another, our loyalty to each other. The way that Robby is standing up to me, which I had first seen as him being defiant, is him being protective... of her and his love for her.

He's acting just like Darry! This is exactly how Darry would have acted had this been us, being caught like this. He would have tried to put himself in front of me and he would have fought tooth and nail for his right to sneak off and kiss me too.

All of my shock and anger melts off of me. I am defenseless, unable to argue any further. I can't help but smile at the thought that he would have acted just like this, as I tell me brother and Beth, "Fine, I get it. I understand. You love each other." I step out from in between the two of them and Robby runs over to take her hand, to which she looks up with a big smile on her sweet girl in love face, and I continue, "I won't tell any of them, but you both have to promise me that you will not be sneaking off to do anything other than kissing! So help me, Robby, if you so much as..."

I stop because of the horrified looks on their faces. I can't stop it from coming out, I'm laughing uncontrollably at their expressions and the fact that Beth just pulled her hand from his just at the thought of anything beyond kissing.

"Ewww!" She cries and turns to run inside my parents' house. Robby looks at me, an annoyed look on his face, "She just agreed to kiss me, Alley, just today... Thanks."

And he turns to walk inside, probably to find Beth and do major damage control.

Kevin walks out the door and comes down to find me. I'm still laughing when he makes it to me. "What was that all about? Beth came running in, her face brighter than a baboon's butt."

I tell him what had happened and what I had said and about her reaction and Robby's revelation that he'd been working on this kiss and she just agreed to it today, when I walked in on it, disrupting their make out session. And now we're both standing here laughing. I make Kevin promise not to say anything to our parent's unless something forces us to tell them.

But by her reaction to the thought of anything more, I think we're safe, for a while anyway.

"I think we need to go back to church, and I'm thinking maybe we should take those two along with us." I tell Kevin, waiting for him to protest, but he agrees and says he thinks that's a great idea.

We walk back to the house, hand in hand, Kevin swinging our arms as we walk. "So, when do you want to ask all of the grandparents' about taking shifts watching Dally while we're gone to Oregon?"

I smile at him, knowing he doesn't want to be the one to do it. "Now's as good a time as any, I'll get this bunch if you'll ask your parents." He nods in agreement and texts his mom.

Once we're inside, I find them all finishing their coffee, almost ready to go back out to tend to the farm, and I peek my head in the door, "Hey, you think y'all would be willing to take shifts staying with Dally, so we don't have to put her on a plane?" I ask, wording it that way on purpose.

They all agree and tell us to let them work out a schedule and they'll get back to us. Kevin comes in telling everyone that his parents agree to take whatever days they are needed on as well.

I cross the room to take Dallas from Mom and kiss her face. "I love you, baby girl. I'll see you this afternoon." I tell her, handing her off to Kevin who does the same. "Thank y'all so much for doing this, and for everything you do to help us and keep us going. Y'all are amazing! Truly." He tells them, taking my hand to lead me out to his truck so we're not late for school.

"Two more weeks! And we're free!" He says, helping me into the truck and closing the door. *Two more weeks, and I'm free.*

CHAPTER TWENTY-SEVEN

It's graduation day, the town is all decorated and lit up; people are so excited and just about everyone has come out to support us. The gymnasium is packed as we all gather on the stage to take our seats for our commencement ceremony. We're all wearing our dark green cap and gown, waiting eagerly to have this done and over with.

None of our group are sitting together, as everything is done in alphabetical order.

The gym is very noisy as excited voices fill the room, echoing off the walls. Moms and dads, grandparents, aunts, uncles, siblings and all kinds of extended family sit staring at us, talking about how proud they are of their student about to take that last walk through high school to accept their diploma and signify and end as well as a beginning in their lives. All I can think about is the fact that Darry isn't here to accept his diploma. Again, something else he was robbed of.

I try my best to shake off the thoughts now dragging me down on a day that should be happy and exciting for me. I scan the crowd, looking for that one face that I need to see to bring me back around. There she is. That light in the darkness, mommy's little love; Dallas is sitting on Bobby's lap, looking at the crowd, smiling at everyone. She turns toward me, and I wave at her. She sees me and smiles, making me forget anything negative or bad.

They begin calling students up and I watch as kids I've known my whole life step into adulthood, leaving behind the childhood that we all shared. We're moving forward, whether we're ready or not. One by one each of us takes our walk across the stage. Families are standing and clapping for their student, so proud of their achievement.

When it's each of our turn to walk, all of our families stand and clap, making a big scene on purpose, hooping and hollering as we walk down the stage to get our diplomas. I watch Dally, looking from each of her grandparents to the other as they act a fool, and she's smiling so big, clapping along with them, kicking her feet as they dangle over her Pawpaw's arms.

It's the cutest thing to watch; her reaction to them; the poor girl not realizing they'll be doing this to her one day too.

When Kevin walks, I feel a lump in my throat, as I fight back happy tears. Kevin, Jessica, Joel and I came a long way in a short time, fighting for our chance to be here today; Joel especially. I am so proud of each one of us.

When it's my turn, I get up to walk, expecting the same thing that the other's got; all of our families' standing up, clapping and making a scene.

Almost the entire audience stands, clapping for me as I make my way across the stage. And I realize immediately that they're not only clapping for me, they're clapping for Darry; these are all people who had their lives touched by my husband in one way or another. It's very evident that this show of emotion is out of respect for him and the life that he never got to finish.

When I get to the other side of the stage and reach my hand out for my diploma, I see the tears in our Principal's eyes. Mrs. Popovitz leans in to hug me and whispers that there's a surprise inside of my diploma, that she has now placed in my hand. I smile and thank her, turning to walk back to my seat.

When the last person takes their walk, and we're all seated back where we started, Mrs. Popovitz announces, "We're proud to present to you the graduating class of 2019!" And we all toss our caps into the air.

After the ceremony, we all come together outside for photos and congratulations. It's a big to-do, with so many families, that we cover the entire front grounds of the school.

I hear of at least three different graduation parties going on tonight, everyone's happy to be finished with school, but sad to be going in different directions now that it's all over. Some of them are leaving for college, traveling as far as New York, and as close as one or two states away.

A lot of us are staying right here, and though Kevin should be pursuing a career in art, he's staying here too, to marry me and help raise Dally. I'm not sure I like the idea of him giving up his dreams for us, but at the same time, I would be lost if he decided to leave to chase after bigger things.

I know it's a selfish thought, and I should want him to go make something more of himself, but I want him to stay and be my husband, and Dally's daddy. We'll be plenty happy on our little pumpkin patch and tree farm, I think.

"Hey, where are you right now?" I hear Kevin's voice break through my thoughts, bringing me into the conversation happening around me. He's holding Dally on his hip, as she tries to grab the tassel hanging down from his cap, laughing every time he moves his head and it swings just out of her reach.

"Huh? Oh, I'm here. I guess I was just thinking of our future." I tell him, and notice him flinch a little, unsure of how different my idea of "our future" may be from his idea of "our future".

"You aren't getting cold feet, now are you?" he asks, a loo of anxiety coming across his gorgeous face.

I reach up to kiss him and tell him, "Not at all, it's nothing like that. We can talk about it later if you want." He nods and we agree to come back to this discussion at another time.

"Congratulations, Mr. Jones." We hear an unfamiliar voice say and turn around to see a gray-haired man in a dark blue suit, with a patch that holds a familiar logo that I can't quite place right now. Kevin turns to the man, greeting him and shaking his hand.
"It's nice to finally get to meet you, Mr. Jones. My name is Frank Messer and I'm from Montana State University. I work as a recruiter for the Academy of Art & Design", he tells us, and I feel my heart begin to sink as Kevin's eyes light up, but then watch as his expression quickly turns to confusion.

"Wait, I haven't submitted anything..." Kevin begins to tell him, trying to figure out how this man even knows about him or about his art.

Kevin looks at me, his expression asking if I did this. I shake my head and shrug my shoulders. He looks to his parents, but they react the same as me.

Mr. Messer continues, "A Mr. Daryl Williams submitted some of your work to us last year, along with a letter asking us to come out and meet with you today. He told us that you would be a wonderful addition to our University's Art Program. The pieces that he submitted inspired me to be here today, as I tend to agree with Mr. Williams, and we'd like to offer you a full scholarship to the Program. If you're interested that is."

The look on Kevin's face is one of confusion, then gratitude to his best friend, then joy and happiness over this opportunity, and then when he sees me and looks down at our daughter, still in his arms; fear and uncertainty.

"I-I don't know. I had not even thought of college." He manages to stammer.

"Is Mr. Williams here with you all today? I'd like to meet this young man." Mr. Messer asks us, looking around as if he'd somehow manage to pick Darry's face out of the crowd.

"No, I'm sorry, but he passed away in a car accident last August." Kevin tells him, looking to me and back to the man standing in front of us, trying to change our lives-again.

"Well, I'm sorry to hear that. I can tell by the letter he sent to me, that he was a great fan of yours and admired you and your ability greatly. I wish I could have met such a person that would look out for a friend's future in such a way."

I see the tears beginning to well in Kevin's eyes and look around at all of the faces standing around us that I love so dearly, all of which now have tears threatening to roll down their cheeks as well.

"Well, Mr. Jones, I don't think I have to tell you what a great opportunity this could be for you. Why don't you think on it for a few days and give me a call when you've made a decision? We'd love to have you." He hands Kevin a card and turns to walk away, leaving all of us speechless and not sure what to think or how to act.

Mary is the first to break the silence, coming over to hug her son, and pat him on the back. "This is a big decision son; you need to take the man's advice and think it over. It could mean big things for your little family here."

Kevin looks down at Dallas and back at me, sensing the anxiety beginning to creep up in the pit of my stomach, he puts his arm around me and pulls me into him, kissing the top of my head. "It's ok, Alley. I'm not going anywhere." He tells me, and I instantly feel bad for him.

He's an amazing artist, one that could go far in that world. But that world isn't our world. Now, I really have to think about some things. Now nothing seems as clear cut as it did just a few moments ago.

CHAPTER TWENTY-EIGHT

When we get home, we change into shorts and tank tops. I sit on the edge of the bed to slip on my sandals and look over at Kevin who's sitting at the foot of the bed, pulling on his tennis shoes. He hasn't really spoken much since the encounter with Mr. Messer. I know this is messing with his head; I can't imagine the way he's feeling right now. He must feel pulled in every different direction, unsure of what he should do. I know I would.

"Kev?" I speak up, needing to clear my throat from being silent for so long.

"Yeah?" He replies, looking over his shoulder at me.

"What are you thinking about?"

He shrugs but doesn't say a word.

"Kev, it's ok to tell me if you're considering his offer. You won't hurt my feelings." I try to assure him.

He lays back on the bed, flat on his back, reaching his arms out to touch me. "Alley, I'm not considering his offer." He says as he grabs my shorts, pulling me toward him on the bed. When I'm right behind him, he lifts his head and lays it on my lap, looking up into my eyes.

"My place is here, with my family. I'm going to plant pumpkins and Christmas trees and we're going to have our own little patch of paradise right here in Cedar Ridge. Besides, how could I go away to school when I'm gonna have six kids to help raise right here?" He says, winking at me, a grin coming up on his lips.

"Six kids?! Kevin Jones, you've lost your ever-loving mind!" I yell at him, surprised that he just said that. He nods and lifts himself up to kiss my lips.

"Yep, six kids. Maybe more. We'll have to see." He says and sits up, getting off the bed and coming around to grab my hands, lifting me to my feet in front of him. He puts his arms around my back and pulls our bodies together. "I want to marry you and be here with you and Dally every day, Alley. I've never wanted to be away from you, even when I couldn't have you." He kisses me again and then pulls my hand above my head, and spins me around, leading me out of the bedroom.

"Now, let's go have some fun!" He says, excitedly, and we leave the house to go find a party.

The first party is at the house of Greta Filch, a girl that neither of us has really ever spent much time with, but she's very popular, so we knew that more than likely, there would be a few people here we'd want to see and say goodbye to before they leave for college.

When we pull up to her house, there are already quite a few cars parked in the driveway, some even on the front lawn. Every light in her very large house is on and we can see people moving around inside through the sheer curtains on the windows.

When we get inside, the music is loud, and the drinks are everywhere. Neither of us drink alcohol, we've just never really seen a reason to get stupid drunk and throw all caution and sense to the wind, as clearly some of our classmates and lifelong friends have chosen to do tonight.

There are a few others drinking water or lemonade, but for the most part, this house is full of underage drunks, with no clue about the horrible decisions they're making and how they will affect them in the morning.

We walk through every room, looking for people that we want to hang with, but unable to find anyone sober enough to really have a conversation with anyway. So, we leave and look for one of the other parties we heard about.

The second party is at the house of a boy named Roger Tanner. Roger is an audio/visual geek (and I say that as a term of endearment and nothing more), that Kevin has been friends with since the fifth grade. They both draw and love art, but they also share a love and obsession with old movies.

When we pull up to Roger's house, which is much smaller than Greta's, we see that it's also much less crowded. We knock and wait to be invited in. When Roger opens the door, his eyes light up at the sight of Kevin standing there, and he invites us in immediately. We're directed to the livingroom, where a small group of people are sitting on the couch, in the dark, watching an old black and white movie, discussing and analyzing the scenes as they go.

I look at Kevin, trying to make him understand that this is not exactly my cup of tea. He seems to understand, but he shrugs and follows Roger into the livingroom anyway, bringing me with him, he sits on the arm of the couch, pulling me onto his lap as he jumps into the conversation as this is obviously a movie he's seen many times before.

After about thirty minutes of this, I excuse myself to the bathroom and begin looking for something to occupy my mind with along the way; a magazine, a book, a pillow and blanket... anything!

Unable to find anything, I use the bathroom and wash my hands. When I turn off the light and step into the hallway, Mark Grayson is standing in the dark right outside the door. When I walk out, he startles me and I jump, putting my back against the wall beside the door. He comes over, standing in front of me and lifts his arms over my head, bracing himself on the wall behind me as he leans in, looking down at me.

I don't know what to do. I have no clue what he's thinking. He has me trapped as he whispers, "Sorry, didn't mean to scare you. I just wanted to talk to you." I can smell the alcohol on his breath. I hadn't even noticed that anyone was drinking. "You know, I always did like you, Alice." He slurs my name, and I realize that he's three sheets to the wind. He leans in closer and before I can react, he's trying to kiss me. I try to break free, but he's got his arms around me, holding me still, unable to do much more than squirm, I pull my lips tightly together, refusing to kiss him back or allow him to kiss me.

Suddenly, Mark is no longer standing in front of me. Someone's grabbed him and pulled him away from me. That same someone has him pinned to the ground and is hitting him in the face repeatedly. The deep thud sound that comes with each blow fills my ears, and then it hits me that it's Kevin. I panic and try to pull him off of Mark. I'm not really trying to save Mark as much as I'm trying to keep Kevin out of trouble. The way he's wailing on this poor guy, he could really hurt him.

"Kevin! Stop! Please, stop!" I say and reach for his arm as it flies up between punches. Without looking at me, he swings his arm backward, pushing me and throwing me into the wall behind us.

I hit my head hard and feel the pain radiate through me. He's to his feet, instantly at my side, trying to make sure I'm ok. "Oh my God, Alice, I'm so sorry. I didn't mean to push you. I was just in the moment. I didn't realize..." he says, pulling me to my feet and wrapping me in his arms.

He pulls away from me, and looks me in my eyes, remorse all over his face, "I'm really sorry, are you ok?" I nod, rubbing the back of my head, feeling the wince of pain shoot down my neck.

"I think I'm done with graduation parties though. Can we just go home now?" I ask, walking by Mark, who's suddenly sober now, trying to figure out why Kevin just handed him his butt.

"Next time you might want to think twice about trying to molest someone in a dark hallway", I say, pushing his leg out of my way with my foot.

I look over at Kevin, who's now looking at me with pride in his eyes. "Really?" He asks, laughing and

shaking his head. "I just pummeled the poor guy; I think he gets it." He says, waving goodbye to Roger and leading me out the front door.

CHAPTER TWENTY-NINE

When we pull into our driveway, we notice Matt's Jeep and Joel's truck are already there. We go inside and they're all four there with Dally, in the livingroom, playing with her on the floor.

"Hey, where are my parents?" I ask them, coming through the door.

"They just left. They were tired, so we told them we've got this." Jess says, handing Dally her stuffed lamb.

"Why are you all here? Didn't you want to go to the parties?" Kevin asks, with levity in his voice over the word "parties".

"Yeah, man, what did you two think about the "parties"?" Joel asks, looking up at me and Kevin.

We drop down on the couch at the same time, look at each and laugh. "What parties? The one that could be called a party was just too much. We're parents now, we don't have time for that. The second party was a bunch of kids sitting around watching an old movie and drinking apparently." I tell them, rolling my eyes, remembering the incident with Mark.

"Yeah, that party turned out to be too much too", Kevin says lifting his fist to show his swollen, bloody knuckles.

"What in the world?" Matt asks, taking Kevin's hand to examine it. "Who did you kill, dude? And why?"

Kevin pulls his hand back, "Man, I didn't kill anybody." He says, acting offended at such an accusation. "Mark attacked Alley when she came out of the bathroom while we were at Roger's house. I had to pull him away from her."

Brittany's eyes are big around as saucers as she listens to the details of the fight.

"Good thing you were there with her. Mark is known for being a little aggressive." She says, her face turning red as she's looking down at the floor.

Matt wraps his arm around her and pulls her to him, but neither of them say anymore.

"So, the party that y'all didn't make it to ended early, when we were all run off by Officer Wiley for noise violation. He had to come out three times before he made us all leave. There wasn't any alcohol though, we were just being loud and rowdy." Matt tells us.

"Yeah, dude, I just don't think that the party life is for us. Even on grad night." Kevin says to them, looking back at me and then to our daughter.

"Have you thought about what you're going to do about the recruiter you talked to today?" Jess asks Kevin.

"I'm staying right here, with my family." He tells her, as if it was a given.

They all look at each other and back to us, "That's great, man. We're all happy for you." They tell us.

"Dally needs her family intact, she needs stability." Brittany adds, brushing a curl away from Dallas's face.

We spend the rest of the evening playing with Dallas, hanging out watching tv and talking. None of us ready to let the night end, none of us sad that we didn't get to have a wild night out. Just a group of friends, that have been through a lot, safe and secure, having fun laughing together in our little sanctuary.

A few days later, Matt calls Kevin and he gets up to take the call privately in our room, which is a bit strange considering they will usually talk about anything in front of me, including all of their guy talk that I would rather not hear.

I sit and finish my coffee, waiting for Dallas to wake up, wondering what could Matt be telling him that needed privacy?

Kevin comes out of our room a few minutes later, "Hey, babe, we're gonna go to dinner with everyone tonight, is that ok?"

It's a bit suspicious, but I agree and call mom to set up a babysitter. "Sorry, honey, me and Daddy already have plans tonight, Elaine and Bobby are going with us, so you'll have to check with Kevin's parents."

"Kevin, can you please check with your mom to see if she can keep the baby tonight?" I ask him. He nods and pulls out his phone to text her.

They agree to keep her, telling us they'll be here around 6pm.

It's Saturday, which is normally everyone's date night, so I know his parents are more than likely breaking a date to keep her. We don't get to have Saturday date nights normally, so I'm very thankful to them for doing it.

We have to go to Henry's for groceries today, so I make a mental note to pick up flowers for Kevin's mom and for his dad, I'll pick up his favorite candy bar.

When Dally's all dressed and ready, we drive to town, ready to fill the fridge and pantry with goodies for the week. Henry's is packed, even for a weekend. When we finally find a parking spot in the tiny lot, we make our way inside to find all four registers open and crowded with long lines.

"I didn't realize there were this many people in this small town", Kevin jokes, putting Dally's carseat in the front of the buggy and locking it in.

"I know, I wonder why everyone's here today", I ask, looking around at all the faces passing by us.

Then we see it. A big makeshift sign is leaned up against the top shelf in the middle of the store; 'Going out of business' is written in big red letters.

"What??" We both say in unison. "Why on earth would the store be going out of business? They're the only grocery around here besides Wal-Mart." Kevin says to me.

"I have no idea. But this is terrible. I really don't like going into Wal-Mart, I'd rather have Henry's any day", I tell him.

We fill our buggy with what we can find from our list and go to check out. Ms. Holly is there at the register, her eyes swollen and red, like she's been crying. Ms. Holly's worked at Henry's for 33 years, this closing has to be hard on her.

"How are you doing, Ms. Holly?" Kevin asks her.

"Oh, I'm alright, I suppose. I'm still breathing, so God has blessed me again today." She says, sniffling.

"What's going on? Why's the store closing?" He asks her, hoping she'll know more than we do.

"Oh, you know, it's those stupid ole' chain stores coming in, setting up shop all around this little town. They're pulling our business and cutting into profit. There's not enough money coming into this little old store anymore to justify keeping it open any longer, I guess."

We tell her how sorry we are, and check out, both of us feeling down, like we're losing something major, and I guess in a way, we are.

"This is horrible", I complain, not wanting to lose the grocery store we've gone to since we were kids. "I agree, but there's nothing we can do." Kevin tells me, saddened by the reality that the outside world is coming to our tiny little town.

We drive home in silence, worried about the sanctity of our little town.

CHAPTER THIRTY

We pull up to the Japanese Hibachi restaurant and park. Matt and Brittany are already waiting outside for us. Kevin comes around to open my door for me, just as Joel flies into the spot next to us. Kevin pushes me back into the car, closing the door, jumping back against it. He hits Joel's door, 'Dang, dude! Watch yourself!" Kevin yells.

"Sorry man, I didn't realize y'all were over here. My bad" He says to Kevin, making sure Kev didn't dent his door. "You didn't have to hit her, dude."

"I had Alley halfway out of the car, you almost hit *her*."

Kevin opens my door again, reaching in to take my hand and help me up. I look at Joel, "Nice driving there, sir."

"Sorry, Alley", he says, looking down and then stepping forward to hug me. "I'm glad I didn't squish you, though." He says smiling, trying to lighten the mood with a not so funny joke.

"Y'all hungry? I'm starving!" Jessica says as she walks around the car to join us. "Thanks for getting my door, dear."

"Sorry about that, glad to see you managed it though." He says, winking at her. Joel knows exactly how to handle Jess and it's fun to watch these two go back and forth. He walks over and puts his arm around her shoulders, walking her toward Matt and Brittany.

Kevin and I follow.

160

"Hey, y'all ready?" Matt asks, opening the door to the restaurant. He's nervous; biting on his bottom lip and playing with the hair on the end of his chin.

I thought something was up, now I'm sure of it… but what? We go inside and walk over a small bridge that takes us over a beautiful koi pond. The vibrant orange and white fish are swimming around, not a care in the world, not even bothered by the sound of our shoes on the wooden bridge beneath our feet. I stop to lean over the railing, wanting to get a better look. Kevin stops too because I'm holding his hand, refusing to take another step forward.

"What are you doing, crazy girl?" He asks, half laughing. His words make me snap to attention. I turn my head to stare back at him, still leaned over the railing. I just smile and turn back. Darry used to call me that all the time; "Crazy girl". It warms my heart to hear it again in such a loving tone.

"Come look", I tell him, pulling his hand, bringing him to the railing with me. "Look how beautiful."

He smiles and kisses my cheek, then he bends over to look into the pond with me. A couple comes in the door beside us and we have to pull into the railing for them to cross the little bridge, but I still refuse to move.

The pond is amazing. There's a bright neon green light under the water causing a green glow over the bottom of the pond, making the water light up neon green. There are light gray and dark gray river stones covering the bottom as well. But it's the rippling water that's really caught my attention. Its soft, slow movement is captivating and relaxing. When the fish swim by, it causes more ripples to be left in their wake, inspiring a deeper trance. I could stand here the remainder of our dinner and not be bothered a bit by missing out on the fire show or the meal.

"Babe?" Kevin starts, "We should probably go to the table now."

I look up at him and he's smiling down at me. I can see the amusement in his expression, and I know he could stay here with me too, but he's right and he knows something.

I agree and he leads us through the restaurant, looking for our friends. When he spots them, he picks up his speed, dragging me behind him. "My legs aren't that long, Kev. I don't walk this fast!" I say, trying to keep up with his long strides. He turns to see me struggling and slows, allowing me to catch my breath and walk at a normal pace for me.

"Thank you."

At the table, he pulls my chair out, allowing me to sit first. He sits next to me and I look around the table. It's not bad, there's only two other couples seated around a table that could easily hold 15-20 people.

"I guess the dinner rush hasn't hit yet" I say pointing out my observation.

Everyone agrees and goes back to their menu.

I decide to order the steak, chicken and vegetables. While Kevin decides he's getting the plate that comes with all of the various meats and vegetables. "You'll never eat all of that", I say, challenging him. "watch me, doll… watch me", he says, sticking his tongue out at me. But I'm quicker than he realizes and grab his tongue, holding it, not allowing him to pull it back into his mouth. "Th-hey, th-top that!" He says. "Sticking your tongue out at someone is rude, mister", I remind him and let go of his tongue, smiling as he looks at me shocked by my behavior.

Just as I turn to talk to Jess, Kev licks up the entire right side of my face. "If sticking my tongue out is rude, I bet that's totally uncalled for, huh?" He asks, laughing at his nasty attack on my cheek and the look on my face.

With eyes peering at him, my jaw shut tight, I wipe my face with a napkin and without saying a word, I turn to him and reach up to pinch his arm.

"Owww!" He cries, rubbing the burning spot on his flesh. "Violence is *never* the answer!" He whines, laughing at the same time.

When I turn back to Jess, I see all four faces looking at us, smiling happily.

"It's great to see you two like this; playful and cheery", Matt says first.

"Yeah man, it feels good to be like old times. Having fun ribbing each other and picking on Alley." Joel says, laughing and leaning over to nudge me.

I look at Kevin and smile and we lean in for a kiss.

"It does feel good to be out, having fun and not having to think too hard about anything too *real*." I admit, putting my hand under Kevin's on the table.

"Well, I hate to make it real then, but I called everyone here for a reason." Matt says, standing up, reaching into his pocket and turning to face Britt. Kevin squeezes my hand, making me look back at him, he smiles and winks, nodding his head toward Matt, like he's telling me, "Watch this."

I turn back to Matt and Brittany, who is shifting nervously in her seat now looking around to each of us, questioning with her eyes if we knew about this. I shrug my shoulders at her and smile, nodding her toward Matt.

He smiles when she looks back in his direction and kneels in front of her, holding up a dark red box and opening it to reveal a gorgeous solitaire diamond ring. She holds her hands together, pulling them to her chest, and looks at the man she loves, kneeled in front of her now. "Yes!" She says, so excited she can't contain herself. "You didn't let me ask." Matt says, laughing. "Oh, sorry. Ask", she tells him, slightly bouncing in her seat.

He shakes his head and laughs again, then he says, "Brittany, I love you so much. I love how sweet you are, and how you love everyone so easily. I love how you smile every time you see me like you haven't seen me in forever. I love how you aren't afraid to put me in my place or pull me in when I go too far. I love how you know me better than anyone else in this world and you still think I'm awesome." He says, crinkling his nose at her. "Britt, please marry me and let me love you forever."

"Yes!" She says, jumping to her feet, throwing her arms around his neck when he stands with her. She's jumping up and down in his arms, making him shake too, while everyone around the restaurant is clapping and laughing with us.

CHAPTER THIRTY-ONE

"So, a double wedding then?" I ask, half joking. Kevin squeezes my hand and smiles. Brittany shrugs and looks at Matt, who then looks from Britt to Kevin and back to me. "Sure, I'm down."

"I was kidding, guys. I didn't really think you'd jump on the idea." I tell them, confused that they'd want to share their day with anyone else.

"Well, we actually have some news for you all too." Jess says, grabbing Joel's hand and looking over at him. I look at Joel, as what she's about to say sinks in. "We're engaged too!" She says, holding up her hand to show off her new ring.

"What?!" We all say in disbelief.

"Why didn't you tell anyone?" I ask, looking around the table to see if anyone truly knew but didn't say anything.

"We wanted to surprise everyone." Joel says, kissing his new fiancés hand.

"Well, it worked, we're surprised", we all say together, laughing, happy for our friends.

"Well, what a night this has turned out to be, huh?" Kevin says, leaning into whisper to me. He kisses my cheek and whispers, "I got the best one, though." I look at him, blushing and he winks at me.

It's nice to be out, away from everything, not stuck in the house. I look around the table as they're bringing out our food and I take it all in. The smiling faces, the love in everyone's expressions. We've all come such a long way since the accident. None of us thought we'd ever be able to smile again; much less be happy like this.

I'm so happy for the people sitting at this table with me. Everyone's in love and finally looking forward to something, big things; major changes are coming for all of us. And I honestly wouldn't mind a triple wedding. These are my friends, my family, I'd be thrilled to share our day together.

"So, we're planning not one, not two, but three weddings." I say, taking a bite of chicken and scooping up a zucchini slice. "This should be fun."

"I don't know, I kind of like the idea of the shared wedding. I love all of you guys, I think it would be cool to have our anniversaries on the same day", Brittany says, looking at Matt. "I mean, what do you think, dear?"

"Yeah, man, I'm up for it. These are my brothers, why wouldn't I say yes?" He says, looking around at Joel and Kevin. Joel reaches over and pats him on the shoulder. "I love you too, man", he says to Matt, winking.

"Jess?" Joel asks, looking at her as she shifts in her seat.

"I mean... I... um, I don't know." She stammers, looking around at each of us, unsure of what to say. I knew she'd be the one to have serious questions; she's never been one for sharing the spotlight.

"It's ok, Jess, if you don't like the idea, that's your right as the bride." Joel says, leaning in to kiss her. "I'll still be there when you walk down the aisle... either way."

She smiles at him and I see her soften immediately. He has some kind of effect on her that no one else has or has ever had. He makes her nicer. It's cool to see him look at her or say something to her and her walls just fall down.

"Yeah, I think I like the idea. Let's do it!" Jess says, leaning in to rub noses with Joel, who smiles at her and puts his hand up to the back of her head, smoothing her hair and leaning his forehead against hers. "I love you", he tells her, and she smiles through flushed cheeks.

CHAPTER THIRTY-TWO

When we leave the restaurant, we leave different than when we walked in. We're bonded a little more, sharing something so intimate, and so life changing, we all feel older, more mature and just closer somehow. Even me and Jess hug before we part ways. For a split second, I hear Darry laughing at us; two girls that were at each other's throats not too long ago, now hugging and promising to get together to go over venue ideas and wedding decorations. I can't help but smile at the thought.

"You know Darry's up in Heaven happy with us right now." I say to her, a half smile on my face. "I mean look at us, making wedding plans together. What a change a year makes, huh?" I tease her.

"Yeah, definitely", she says, grabbing my elbow and moving me away from the rest of the group. "Look, I'm really sorry for how I treated you before. I was a real jerk, Alice. You didn't do anything to deserve that, and I really hate that we lost all that time because I couldn't get myself straight. I love you, you're one of my very best friends... no, my sister. But if you tell anyone I said any of that, I'll find you and kill you." She says, smiling at me and then hugging my neck.

"I love you too, Jess. I'm so glad we're sisters."

Kevin comes over and puts his arm around my shoulders, kissing the side of my head. "You over here trying to steal my girl away or what?" He says to Jess, winking at her. "Eat your heart out, Kevin Jones!" She says and turns to sashay away over to Joel.

"What was that about?" Kev asks me as we walk to the car.

"Oh nothing, just wedding stuff, babe", I say and look back at Jess, who smiles and nods at me.

"You're so beautiful, Alley. I'm so lucky that you love me." He tells me, unexpectedly. His expression very serious, but soft.

"Wow, thank you. But I'm the lucky one, babe. I'd be lost without you." I assure him, snuggling into his chest as he embraces me, pulling me to him.

"I think we're all lucky", he says, smiling over my head at our friends now getting into their own vehicles, ready to drive off together.

And I have to agree.

It's not often you find love in this life; not real - honest to God, overwhelming, all consuming, passionate love, but luckily, we all have. And I was lucky enough to find it twice.

For a fleeting moment, I catch a glimpse of an emotion that I haven't had since I was a child; like I'm seeing the world through new eyes and I can feel the magic in the air, all over my skin, running through me, leaving behind a sudden jarring electrical current that runs through my veins, making my head feel all tingly.

I get into the car as Kevin opens my door, feeling oddly at peace with myself, with him, with everything. There's nothing negative, no bad thoughts or lingering painful emotions; just love and warmth, adoration and respect, calm and a peacefulness deep in my heart that I haven't known in so long.

"I can't wait to get home to see Dallas", I tell Kevin as he sits next to me. He looks at me and smiles as he pats my knee.

"Me too, babe, it feels like we've been away from her for days, doesn't it?"

I nod in agreement and wonder to myself what that's about. We were both so eager to have a night out and now we can't get home fast enough.

We kiss her cheek and finish packing for our trip. I don't know how we'll manage to be away from her for a whole three days, it's going to be tough.

"We'll have to video chat with her, you know?" I mention to Kevin while we're shoving socks and underwear into our suitcases.

"Yeah, I know. This is going to be hard. Three days away, and not just away from her, but states away, is going to be impossible." He says, walking over to rub her back. She squirms and we look at each other with the fear of God on our faces. "Don't wake her up now", I whisper. "I've got to get some sleep before our flight tomorrow!" I scold him.

The next morning, we wake up early with an hour to spend playing with Dally. She's in an especially chipper mood, laughing and falling back on the floor so she can put her toes in her mouth.

"What are you doing there, little one?" Kevin asks her, lifting her back up to a sitting position and propping her against a pillow. "You don't have to eat your cute little toes, we can afford to feed you mushy bananas and custards, ya know?" He tells her and laughs as she shifts her body, making herself fall back again and sticking her toes right back into her mouth.

"You're so silly!" I tell her, tickling her belly, listening as her sweet laugh fills my ears.

The front door opens, and Jess and Joel come walking into the livingroom. "Morning" Joel says as Jess groans and without saying a word, plops down, laying her head on a pillow, pulling her legs into her chest. "She's still half asleep", he says, nodding toward his now snoring fiancé laying on our couch. "She's no good before 10am lately."

We all laugh, and Joel comes to sit on the floor with us. "We are very grateful to you two for staying with her. I was going to try to do this on my own, but I don't think I can. I need Kev with me." I tell them again, as if they haven't heard this same speech over and over the past two days, while I try to convince myself that this is ok, we are doing the right thing by leaving our child here and not putting her on a plane.

"It's ok, Alley. I promise that we've got this. And tonight, Matt and Britt will be here too. I think the four of us can handle her and your parents are right there", he says pointing toward my parents' house.

I nod and hug him, thanking him again. Kevin stands up and reaches for my hand, "I think we should get a move on, my dear. We don't want to miss our flight."

He helps me to my feet, we kiss Dally one last time before we head out the front door, listening to Joel talk sweetly to her, playing on the floor with her. He's a great Uncle to her. I feel anxious leaving her, but I know she's in good hands. And when Jess wakes up, she'll have even more love showered on her.

We load the trunk of my car and drive off toward the airport, me holding the tiny little urn of Darry's ashes in my lap.

CHAPTER THIRTY-THREE

The airport is packed when we arrive. We park and grab our things, running for the door, hoping to make it through security checks in time to make our flight. We pass blurry faces as we run through the terminal, only stopping once we reach security. They go through our bags, painstakingly slow, making me happy with our decision to bring as little as possible.

They try to give me a hard time abut bringing Darry's urn onto the plane, but I am somehow able to talk them into giving me a pass; maybe they felt sorry for the too young to be a widow girl standing in front of them, who knows? I'm not one to question their reasoning, I thank them, and we walk on through.

We make it to the boarding area right as they're starting to close the door. Kevin hollers for her to hold the door and she stops, opening the door to allow us through, only stopping us long enough to take out tickets.

We get to the plane and take our seats. Thankfully we're in seats that sit next to a window. Last time I was on a plane, Darry let me have the window seat and it really helped to calm my nerves about flying. I look to Kevin, questioning him with my eyes, and he moves aside allowing me to take the seat that I prefer.

We begin to roll down the runway and Kevin looks over at me, smiling. "Nervous?" He asks, taking my hand in his and kissing it. I hadn't even noticed I was grasping the arm of the seat so hard, until he pried my fingers from it. "I don't like the "whoosh" feeling in my belly when we take off, that's all", I tell him, trying to give him my best possible smile.

He nods in understanding and puts his arm around my shoulder, allowing me to lay my head on his chest as we take off into the clouds. Once the plane steadies, I look out the window and see the tiny terminal beginning to get smaller and smaller until I can't see it anymore. There is nothing but blue sky and clouds around us now; it's incredibly beautiful and calming actually. Kevin leans over me, looking out the window, taking it all in, his green eyes getting bigger and then smaller as he tries to make out anything on the ground below us. Unable to see anything really, he sits back and settles into his seat, closing his eyes.

We sleep through some of the flight, exhausted from the night before and the lack of real sleep that came from nerves over leaving Dally.

I wake up sometime before we land and find Kevin awake, holding his phone in front of him, headphones in. I peer over at the small screen and see that he's watching a broadcast of Pastor Rainey's sermon from this morning. He looks over at me and smiles but doesn't stop the broadcast.

When we land in Oregon, we collect our things and head off to our hotel. I booked a different hotel than the one Darry and I had stayed in because it just felt awkward to even think of staying in our honeymoon hotel with my new fiancé.

The hotel we're staying in isn't far from the other one, but it's not as nice; it's still a great place, and still right on the beach, thankfully. I wanted to be right there again, so we could spend some time enjoying the sounds of the waves and the seagulls.

It's been almost a full year since I was here with Darry, but it feels more like years. So much has happened, so much has changed; I'm not even the same person that I was then.

We put our things in our room and call to let Joel know we made it safely, and to check on Dally. When we are satisfied that she's ok, we head down to the water. This side of the beach is much more crowded than the side that I was on last time. We manage to find a spot to sit down and begin to watch the people around us. They're playing in the water, splashing and laughing; every now and then you'll hear someone scream out in shock as they're pulled into the cool water, but it's immediately followed by happy squeals and joyful chatter.

I look to my right when I hear a baby begin to coo and feel a sudden pang of regret grow in my belly. "Maybe we should have brought Dally", I tell Kevin, still watching the chubby baby play happily on the blanket next to her mommy and daddy. I look back at Kevin as he sees why I am wishing we had our daughter with us. "I miss her too, but I think we were right by not bringing her on the plane." He tells me, asking if I want to go put my toes in the water.

We leave our tiny little spot on the sand and walk toward the water. We're not too far from their pier and when I look down to see it, I notice there's a lot of commotion with a bunch of people standing around. They're filming. "Oh! Look, Kevin!" I say, excitedly, while I'm hitting his arm. He rubs his arm and looks at me and then to the pier.

"What is it?" He asks, squinting his eyes, trying to see what's going on.

"They're filming a movie or something. Look at the cameras and lifts, and the two people standing at the end of the pier." I tell him, trying to get him as excited as I am.

But he isn't impressed, he's more interested in getting me into the water. He comes over to me, sweeps me into his arms and walks into the cold water. I squeal when the water hits my warm flesh, raising goosebumps all over my body.

Kevin laughs and locks his arms around me, pulling me into him. He's in a kind of sitting, kind of not sitting position, squatted down in the water, allowing me to sit on his knees as he walks us around.

"I'd really like to kiss you right now, but there are too many people around; too many kids. Including the one that hasn't stopped watching you since we came into the water." He says, laughing and nodding toward a little blonde-haired boy sitting on the beach with his feet in the water. He's sitting at the water's edge, allowing the waves to come up and cover his feet and then pull back out into the ocean surrounding us. But he's also staring at me, a small smile across his face. He can't be more than 9 years old, and he looks so sweet.

I turn to look at Kevin and smile at him, "Jealous, are we?" I tease him. I put my arms around the back of his neck and lock my fingers into each other, then pull back and drop my head back into the water. When I come back up, he asks me, "I don't know, do I have competition?" He winks at me and looks over at the little boy, but he's not there anymore.

I'm just about to lean in to kiss Kevin when I feel a small, gentle tap on my shoulder. "Excuse me", a tiny little voice says. I turn around quickly and come face to face with the adorable little blonde-haired boy from the beach.

"Yes?" I ask, intrigued and surprised that he came out into the water alone.

"Are you an angel?" The little boy asks me, a small smile starting to crinkle up on the corners of his mouth. I know exactly where this is going but I have to admit, I'm impressed, so I answer him, playing along.

"No, why do you ask sweetie?"

"Because Heaven just called and reported one missing", the little boy said, and turned to swim back to the shore. Me and Kevin look at each other and burst out laughing.

"That little player has got a lot of nerve coming out here to hit on my woman, and with you locked around me too!"

Still laughing I look at the shore and see that he has taken his place right back where he was earlier. Only now he's got an older man sitting with him, that must be his dad. When the little boy sees me looking, he smiles and winks at me. Sending me and Kevin back into hysterics.

"Oh, his dad is gonna have to watch him closely, that one's gonna be trouble!" I tell Kev, as he swings me around, taking my attention from the boy and putting it right back on him. I start to say something, and he locks his lips to mine, kissing me without hesitation, without reason, he pulls me close to him, as if he's reminding me that I belong to only him.

CHAPTER THIRTY-FOUR

I take Kevin around the little town, showing him all of the same places that Darry and I had seen and visited. When he tells me that he's starting to get hungry, I know exactly where to take him and before long we're feeding scraps to stray cats. The memories are bittersweet, and after a while I feel them beginning to weigh on me.

"I think I'm ready to go back to the room, Kev. I'm not feeling so well." I tell him, trying to hide the sadness that's taking over my heart.

"Yeah, ok, let's head back. I'm feeling kind of tired myself."

When we get back to the room, we take turns changing into pjs in the bathroom. There's one king bed in the room, and even though we're used to sharing a bed, it just feels oddly wrong here in this place. Kevin and I haven't done anything beyond kissing, he's been a perfect gentleman all this time, but being here where I honeymooned with Darry, and now sleeping next to his best friend, it somehow feels icky.

I scoot to my side of the bed and hug one of the pillows close to me, avoiding cuddling with Kevin tonight. "Are you ok?" He asks, trying to scoot closer to me. "Alley?" He says when I don't answer him right away.

I turn toward him and look him kin his beautiful, sweet eyes. "I'm ok. I just feel weird being in the bed with you like this when this is where I honeymooned with Darry, that's all." I tell him, trying to be as open and honest as possible with him.

"I understand, babe. Do you want me to sleep on the couch then?" He asks, pointing to the couch that lines the room under the window. I shake my head, feeling silly and cuddle up to him.

"I know this must be very weird for you, Alley. I'm not wanting to make any of this harder on you. I'm here for emotional support, remember?" He says, reminding me that I am the one that asked him to come along on this trip.

I smile and kiss him goodnight.

I can feel the heat before I see the flames. As I walk closer to the house, I see the red-hot flames licking at the curtains, pulling them in and blowing them back out through the busted glass in the windows. The front door is wide open so I can see straight down the hall, where the flames haven't yet reached. Then I hear screaming and a baby crying, as the fire grows, taking over the left side of the house.

"Alley!! Wake up, Alley! Oh man, Alllleeey!"

I snap awake, shaking my head, trying to get the voices in my mind to stop screaming.

"Alley, please wake up. Please stop screaming." I hear Kevin pleading with me, but I don't understand what he means. I'm not screaming... am I? Kevin locks his arms around me, pulling me into him and the screaming stops.

I feel the wet tears on my cheeks, and I can't stop shaking. I'm shaking so hard that I'm making Kevin shake with me as he holds on to me for dear life.

"Alice, what was it?" He asks, knowing it had to have been a bad nightmare, and understanding by now that my dreams usually mean something more.

"Oh, Kevin! It was so awful! The house was on fire, and everyone was still inside!! Please call them, please call Joel, Kevin." I beg him.

"Alley, it's 3am in Montana. They're all asleep." He reminds me, trying to reason with me.

"I don't care, Kevin! Call him! Now!" I scream at him, wanting him to understand that something's not right.

He agrees and picks up the phone, dialing Joel. The phone rings and rings, but no one answers.

I pick up my phone and dial Jess, who answers on the third ring with a very sleepy, "Hello?"

"Hey, Jess, is everything ok?" I ask her, hearing the desperation in my own voice.

"Yeah, we're fine. Why? What's going on? Is something wrong?" I hear the fear in her voice, and I begin to understand that it was just a nightmare, everyone is ok. "I'm sorry, Jess. I had a nightmare. I am so sorry to wake you. I'll talk to you more about it tomorrow, go back to sleep."

"Ok, Alice. Talk to you tomorrow." She says, and we both hang up.

I fall back onto Kev's chest and begin sobbing. I heard my baby's cries as the fire took her. It was the most horrible, heart wrenching thing ever, even if it was just a nightmare. Kevin wraps his arms around me, pulling my back closer to his chest and kisses the top of my head. "It's ok, baby, it was just a nightmare, I'm here and everyone is safe." He quietly hums, rocking me gently until I fall back to sleep.

The next morning, I'm exhausted and worn out from the chaos of the night before, but today is the day that I have to say goodbye to my love, so I get up and get dressed in my best summer dress, the one he loved; the white one with the little purple flowers all over it, and I pull on my boots.

I go to the bathroom and curl my hair, locking it in place on top of my head with a little black barrette.

Kevin is already dressed and sitting out on the patio with a cup of hot coffee, watching the sun come up, listening to the waves come in. He looks so peaceful, and so handsome, sipping from his mug, his eyes fixated on the colors dancing across the horizon.

I slide open the glass patio door and step out when he turns to look at me. He sits his cup down on the glass tabletop and stands to walk over to me, pulling me into him, he leans down and kisses me then he lifts his face to mine, leaning in to put our foreheads together, "Good morning, beautiful. How are you feeling?"

"I'm ok. Kind of nervous about what we're about to do. I'm not sure I'm ready for this, but I know I need to do it." I tell him.

"I understand. Just let me know when you're ready and I'll go get us a car."

I sit for a few minutes on the patio with Kevin, sipping coffee and trying to talk myself into this next part of the trip. Yesterday it was easier to pretend this was a vacation for me and Kevin, a pleasurable trip to the beach. This morning I can no longer hide from the reality of this "vacation". I have to say goodbye to Darry; I have to let him go.

After a few minutes, I feel the moment come that says, "get up and do this now or you are going to sit here forever", so I tell Kevin to go get the car, and I'll meet him out front.

He leaves the room, and I walk over to the nightstand where Darry's little urn is sitting. I sit down on the bed and take the urn into my hands. I can't speak, I don't have the right words. I just hold him to my chest and cry.

Kevin sends me a text telling me that he's downstairs and he's so sorry, but he doesn't say why.

I grab a shawl and my purse and carry myself and Darry out of this room and into the last day that we'll spend together. After today, I will do my best to move on, to move forward without a large portion of my heart.

When I step out of the front lobby doors onto the sidewalk, my breath catches in my throat. In front of my, under the awning of the hotel, is a cherry red Mustang convertible. Kevin is standing beside it, a look of pity and apology on his face.

He rushes over to me, and instantly apologizes, again and again. "Alley, it was all they had. I begged, I even tried to bribe the manager into letting me rent his personal car, but he wouldn't budge. I am so so sorry."

I don't speak a word, I just put my hand out for the keys, and he drops them into my palm. I sit Darry's urn in the backseat and buckle it in. I walk around to the driver side door and get in, nodding for Kevin to take the passenger seat. "Let's go", I tell him, turning the ignition and hearing the familiar roar of the engine.

I know immediately where to go, and how to get there.

We ride along the coast, headed toward the same route that Darry and I had taken to get to the Aquarium last year.

The same familiar scenes pass by us, the ocean, the rock formations, and the lighthouses.

But I'm waiting for one particular spot, one rock formation that stood out to the both of us and had made us feel like kids again. When I see it, I pull the car over to the side of the road, careful to hug as close to the shoulder as possible without putting us in danger.

I step out onto the street and walk around to grab the urn. "Kev, please wait here", I tell him when I see him start to open his door to follow me. "I'll be back in just a few minutes, I promise, but I have to do this part alone." I tell him, begging him to understand.

He nods and sits back down, pulling the door closed behind him.

I walk out to the edge of the cliff, and sit down, letting my legs dangle below me. I turn to put Darry's urn on the ground beside me and we just sit, overlooking the famous rock formation from our favorite childhood movie. The famous quote ringing through my ears, reminding me of days spent on my parent's livingroom floor, eating popcorn, drinking cherry soda and watching the movie over and over again, until we drove my parent's mad.

My memory shifts to us driving up the coast on our honeymoon, us seeing this very spot and freaking out when we realized what it was.

I look out over the ocean and then up to the sky and begin speaking to my husband,

"I love you, Darry. I'll never stop loving you. I'll never stop wishing you were here with us. But I have to let you go for now, babe. I pray you understand, and I hope you'll still be there to hold me when I say my last goodbyes to this place. I know you loved me and Dallas, and I know that you loved Kevin too. I hope that everyone is right, and you are ok with this. I do love him, Darry. It'll never be the same love that we shared, but he loves me, and Dally and he's been such a rock for us. He helped me find the strength to live again when all I wanted was to follow you. He reminded me that I had a piece of you still here that needed me, Darry. He kept me from giving up. I'm saying goodbye to you today, and then I'm going home and I'm going to marry Kevin. But I know that you'll never really be gone from me. If there's such a thing, Darry, haunt me. Stay with us. Watch over us. If not, please know that you are with me, in every breath I take, in the smile and laugh of our daughter, in the heart of everyone who's life you ever touched. You are still here with us, and we will never forget you, Darry."

The tears are streaming down my face as I pick up his urn and kiss it, opening the top, I reach in and grab the plastic bag that holds the remains of my best friend, my husband and the father of my child. I open the bag and reach in, taking a handful of ash, I lift my hand into the air and toss them into the ocean below me, shouting, "Never say die!"

I sit for a few more minutes, crying and remembering my husband before I get up and dust myself off, turning to walk up the hill to the car where my future husband is now watching me. I take the first step and hear Darry's voice carry over the wind, resting on my ears, "I love you, babe. It's ok. Please just live and be happy, for me."

I feel warmth surround my body and as the wind sweeps my hair up above my head, I spin in the warmth, arms put to my sides, my head back as the sun kisses my skin. Peace washes over me and I am instantly released from any doubts about marrying Kevin and moving on without Darry.

I run up the hill, a huge smile across my face. Kevin, now outside, standing next to the car, is looking at me like he's wondering if I've lost my mind. "Are you o..." He starts to ask, but I've already latched onto him, and am kissing him hard.

He manages to pull back and free himself of the unsolicited attack, "Whoa! What just happened?" He asks, confused, and a little shaken.

"We just got Darry's blessing!" I shout into the wind, happy to be free of the inner torment that I've been trying so hard to live with, doing my best to hide it from everyone I love.

"Oh, did we now?" He asks, smiling at me, putting his arms around my back at my waist and pulling me into him, leaning down to kiss me back, matching my earlier enthusiasm.

"Well, shall we go home to our daughter then and start planning our wedding?" He asks, a big smile on his relieved face.

"Yes, sir! Let's go home!" I tell him, ready to leave, even if it is a day early.

CHAPTER THIRTY-FIVE

When we get to the airport, we are told that we can't exchange the ticket for an earlier flight. We'll have to wait to see if someone wants to trade seats on an earlier plane or just wait until tomorrow morning and use the tickets we have already.

We have already given up our room so we can't go back there. Instead we decide to stay in the airport, talking to people and asking if they'd like to trade seats. When we finally realize it's not going to happen, we find two seats to settle into for the remaining few hours left until our flight. We sit down and lean on each other to sleep for a bit.

I'm standing on my front porch, the flames are licking up around my face, the heat is burning me, and I can feel my flesh peeling away. But I've got to get inside, I have to find her. I step into the house and my feet sink into the carpet, like stepping into a giant roasted marshmallow. I try to lift my foot, trying so hard to make it down the hallway that's now stretched out in front of me, but I can't pull my feet out of the melted carpet. I stand there, frozen and burning, unable to do anything but scream.

I feel hands shaking my body. My eyes snap open and I see the fear and anxiety on Kevin's face. His mouth is moving, but nothing is coming out. He's frantic, terrified even. There are two security guards standing behind him and a small crowd is gathering around us. I can see everyone, but there is not a sound around me. Kevin is shaking me by my shoulders, he's screaming at me, but I can't hear his words.

The female security guard pushes Kevin aside with her shoulder, knocking him out of the way, as she steps forward to stand in front of me, she takes me by my shoulders and suddenly I hear the screaming, the blood curdling screams are now piercing my ears. She reaches her arm up above my head and comes down across my cheek, hard. I feel the sting and the screaming stops. Tears are streaming down my face as I am now fully aware of all that's happening around me.

Kevin is on his feet, next to me, he's pulling me up into his arms, hugging me tight. The security guards are visibly shaken, as they take a seat next to us, the lady is shaking her head, her face is bright red.

"That is some scream you've got there, young lady." The male security guard says to me, putting his arm around the female that's just slapped me. "I've never heard anything like it." She tells him.

I sit back down and put my face in my hands, as the crowd around us begins to dissipate, losing interest now that the shows over. "I'm sorry. I'm so sorry", I repeat over and over, humiliated by my actions.

"Young lady, you have nothing to apologize for. I can only imagine the horrors you must have been facing for you to howl like that." The female officer says to me. "I'm sorry for lapping you, but this young man couldn't get it to stop."

I nod at her, understanding full well why she felt compelled to smack me. Kevin is sitting next to me, his arms around my shoulders. He pulls me into lay my head on him and he kisses the top of my head. "We have got to get you in to see someone about this, Alley. You can't keep going like this." He tells me, seriously worried for me.

The plane ride home was uneventful, thankfully. No nightmares, even though I tried hard to stay awake through most of the flight, I had fallen asleep, but it was peaceful enough.

When we get to the car and begin to pull out of the parking lot, I turn our phones back on they both begin to go crazy. Everyone is texting us, we each have 20 or more missed calls. I begin to panic as I dial my mom's number.

Her phone rings and rings, with no answer. Kevin begins calling Joel and Jess, but neither of them answer either. I try Britt and he calls Matt, when we finally get an answer, Kevin puts Matt on speaker phone, as we both bombard him with questions, "What's going on, man?" Kevin asks as I'm also saying, "Matt, is everyone ok?"

We hear chaos and commotion in the background and realize by the sounds coming through the speaker that he's at the hospital. We both get frantic, "What in the world is happening, Matt? Where's Dallas?!" We both scream into the phone. Our heads spinning in fear, our hearts pounding out of our chests, as Kevin flies toward the hospital.

"She's in ICU. We're all here, I'm so sorry, man. You need to get here as quickly as possible, but Kevin, slow down, it's not going to do anyone any good if you kill you and Alley trying to get here." He hangs up the phone and Kevin slows down a bit.

I look down, tears streaming, and whisper, "It's the dream, Kevin. It's my nightmare."

I look over at him when he doesn't say anything, and see he's crying but he's trying hard to focus and get us to our baby, quickly but safely, just like Matt said.

When we get to the hospital, we both jump out of the car, and head for the doors, entering a corridor that we've come to know all too well. We look around for signs of any familiar face we can find.

When we enter a second waiting room, we finally lock eyes with a familiar face; Kevin's dad.

We look around the room and see that his mom is in the corner, she's leaned over, talking on the phone, crying.

Kevin crosses the room to throw his arm around his dad's neck. "What's going on, Dad? Where is she, where is everyone else?" Kevin's voice breaks as he tries to make sense of all of this, he begs his dad to give him any information he can.

His dad sits him down and motions for me to come sit next to him, as he begins to explain to us that there was a fire in our house. The toaster had malfunctioned and caused an electrical fire in the walls of the kitchen that spread quickly and quietly through the front part of the house.

Joel had woken up first to the smell of smoke. He woke up Jess and she had made a bee-line for the baby; crossing through the fire to get to Dally. Joel then woke up Matt and Britt, who ran out of the house to get my parents.

"They're all ok, they got lucky. They all made it out safely, with minor burns. They have Dally in ICU though because the fire started on her side of the house and she inhaled a lot of the smoke. She was having trouble breathing when they got here, so they're checking her out now." Kevin's dad tells us, "We're all just shaken up but relieved too, because it could've been so much worse."

"Where is she, can we see her?" Kevin asks, before I have a chance to.

He nods and tells us to follow him. He leads us to the elevators and pushes the number 4, the burn unit and ICU. When the doors open, we all head for the nurses' station in front of us. They bring us straight back to her room, where she's laying in a big metal crib, hooked up to all kinds of beeping machines. My parents are fast asleep; my mom on the couch by the window, my daddy in the recliner next to the crib, with his head on the mattress beside her, and his hand holding hers.

Kevin and I rush to her side, and peer down over the tall railing that's still up on this side of the bed. Kevin's dad reaches down underneath and lowers the railing for us, so we can touch her. She looks so small and fragile lying there in that big crib, an oxygen mask over her tiny little face and an IV in her little arm.

Her chest is rising and falling but it's catching in between breaths. She's struggling to breathe even now, even with the oxygen. Kevin bends down and kisses her cheek and her eyes flutter open. She doesn't cry or move much; she just looks at us. I kiss her forehead and my tears fall on her face. She closes her eyes and goes back to sleep.

Kevin has the nurse bring us chairs and we pull up next to her crib, watching her sleep, her chest fighting to rise and fall in a satisfying rhythm. Kevin holds my hand as I hold hers, his other hand gently rubbing up and down her little leg.

Matt comes in the room a few minutes later, and we can smell the smoke on his hoodie.

He crouches down between our chairs, leaning on the arms of both chairs, he looks at Kev and whispers, "Hey man, I'm glad y'all made it here in one piece. I just left Jess, she's down in the ER with Joel and Britt. Jess literally ran through the fire as it started to bellow out of the kitchen into the hallway, dude. Her legs and her right arm are burned – I think they said second degree burns, they're treating her now."

He continues, "We all thought the worst when they didn't come back through the hallway. We were outside freaking out on the front porch. By the time we got out there, there was no way we could get back into the house and look for either of them. We were having trouble breathing from the smoke and when the windows blew out, we had to run from the house." Our eyes were wide as we listened to him recant the horrible events that had taken place earlier this evening, while we were flying home.

"Jess broke the bedroom window out in Dally's room and lowered her out wrapped in one of her blankets, man." He tells Kevin, looking down at the floor, shaking his head as he remembers the fear he just faced. He looks at me and whispers, "She went back in for the picture over Dally's bed, Alice. She got it out, man, for Dally."

Tears are streaming down his face. "And for Darry, dude. For Darry."

That's when it hits me. How much did we lose? I'm so happy that everyone got out and no one was lost, but what all was lost? Do we have anything of Darry to give to his daughter now? Are all of our photos gone? All of his stuff, his clothes, his trophies, his colognes that still sit in our bathroom… is it all gone?

I'm so thankful to Jess for getting Dally out and for grabbing that frame for her. That may just be the only picture she has left of her daddy.

CHAPTER THIRTY-SIX

I'm sitting on the front porch watching Kevin and Daddy work the pumpkin patch. It's been four years since the fire took our home and everything we owned. We were able to salvage a few things from the rubble; Darry's Varsity jacket had been spared by what can only be explained as a miracle from God. Kevin's Bible did not burn, the Bible was sitting on the end table by the couch in the livingroom; the fire consumed everything but the Bible. There were some photos in a metal safe that were spared, but the ones that Kevin had hidden for me during my darkest times after losing Darry, had been burned up in the fire.

I was so thankful to Jess for saving the frame that hung up over Dally's bed. I'm still grateful to her; and the frame still hangs over her bed, it's just a twin bed now instead of a crib.

She's grown so much these past few years; and she's a little pistol. This little girl got all of my sass and Darry's quick wit. She doesn't take anything off of anyone, she's quick to put someone back in their place when they step out of line, but then she'll crawl up in your lap and give you the best hugs and kisses.

Kevin and I have been married for almost four years. We got married right after the fire. We had the triple wedding, so we all share an anniversary, which is really cool and convenient for getting together and celebrating, we all only have to remember one date.

The wedding was in the park in the middle of town on a cool Autumn afternoon. We decorated in Fall colors and carried Fall colored bouquets, Jess, Britt and I wore soft, white flowy ankle length gowns, with burnt orange flower accents crawling down the back. The guys wore white tuxes with burnt orange cover buns, vests and ties.

It was a different experience than my wedding to Darry had been. It was less intimate but more so all at the same time. I was standing with the people I love most in this world, sharing our vows, taking the biggest step possible in our relationships; together. We shared the floor for our first dances, and we cut our cakes together. It was such a beautiful experience; one that we will all share and look back on with love, always.

Daddy, Kevin's dad, Frank, and Bobby all had to rebuild our home. We stayed with Kevin's parent's while it was being completed. Since we were starting from scratch, we were able to have more say in it than Darry and I had had.

The house is still a beautiful farmhouse, but with the insurance money, we were able to add an upstairs and a bit more storage space. Kevin and I want a large family, so we added more rooms than we originally had.

I had very specific details that I wanted to add to the home. My porch is my favorite place on the whole house. I asked for a wrap around porch, but I wanted it to be sectioned off in a way that would allow for a summer porch and a winter porch. The front is open to the elements, but then there's a screen door that allows you to enter a screened in porch.

I have my white rocking chairs on the outer porch because that's where I sit most often to watch Dally when she's playing in the yard.

My kitchen is my second favorite place. The big wide window that sits behind the sink, overlooks the pumpkin patch, where Kev and Daddy are working now. I can wash dishes and watch Kevin working hard outside, which is something that I really enjoy doing.

Four years have only added to Kevin's handsome good looks. At 22 years old, he's in the best shape he's ever been in, something that I contribute to his hard work on the farm, and to his new hobby of working out every other day at the local gym with Matt and Joel. It's kind of become their little thing; their down time, to escape their life of responsibilities and stresses. It does them all good to be able to get together to hangout and cut up without any of their wives or kids around to bug them.

Brittany and Matt have two kids, Nathan is just about to be four years old and Bella is 2. Jess and Joel have a newborn baby girl, Madeline; she's only three weeks old and already spoiled rotten by her daddy.

Kevin and I are expecting our son any day now. I am so pregnant right now that I can barely bend down to tie my own shoes; I usually just have Dally do it for me. She thinks it's funny that Mommy can't bend down because she's "fat".

We're thrilled to be adding another member to our family. We tried from our honeymoon, but it took a long time. We spent a lot of time hoping and being disappointed, a lot of tears shed, a lot of prayers went up.

Kevin had already begun going to church before we got married. His mom and dad had talked him to going when we were separated, and he just never left. It took our struggle to have another baby for him to convince me to go.

I wouldn't trade it for anything now. I love my Sunday's in church, our Wednesday night meal and fellowships are something that I look forward to every week. We even dragged Matt and Britt along with us who then turned around and talked Joel and Jess into coming. Now we're all involved and raising our children in Christ.

I teach Sunday school and Jess and Britt are in the nursery, mostly because Jess refused to let anyone else take care of Maddie.

Matt and Britt invested in an old run-down property on the other side of my parent's farm, so we're neighbors. They took the place and opened the field behind their house so that it's all part of the same field that runs beside our house. Matt, Kevin and Daddy are business partners now. Our land tripled when Matt joined his farm to ours, allowing us to turn all of our farms into something really special. We have bouncy houses and hayrides, a small corn maze for the kids, pony rides and sponsored events, like pie eating contests, bake offs, chili competitions as well as barrel races and jumping competitions.

At the beginning of every Fall, we turn the fields into a walk through the Tribulation, where people can come see a live action version of the book of Revelation in a sort of spooky trail. It's a very big event; we have a great turn out, people come from all over the state.

During Christmas we open the tree farm. Me and the girls, including Mom and Elaine and Kevin's mom, Barbra, all run a Christmas Giftshop that the guys built for us because we wanted to have a hand in the business. It does really well for us and with all of the things we have going on with our business, we do very well for ourselves.

It's nice to be able to come to work and not have to leave home, not have to hire a babysitter, or worry about where the kids are and what they're doing. We bring them with us, and they run around the farm while we work. Dally and Nathan are the oldest. They usually help out in the pumpkin patch in the Fall, the tree farm in the Winter or in the shop with us. Sometimes they'll go down to Daddy's farm and help out with the horses and their events, but they mostly like to stay up in patch.

Dally and Nathan remind me a lot of me and Darry. Dally was still just a baby when we found out that Britt and Matt were expecting Nathan. Dally's just at a year older than he is, so she doesn't remember her life before him. They've grown up together just how Darry and I did. We've even woke up in the middle of the night to find Dally gone from her bed, out of the house and over at Nathan's.

The first time that happened, we were all in a panic, outside in the middle of the night, lanterns in hand, calling for her, frantically searching the tree lines between the properties. Matt had gone in to ask Nathan if he had heard from her when he found her curled up in Nathan's bed with him, both of them sound asleep. That had broken my heart a little but warmed it as well. I'm glad they have each other and that their bond is so strong. I know how they feel about each other; I've felt it.

Wherever one of them is, you can be sure the other will be. We never have to look far for either of them. It's the sweetest thing.

Speaking of childhood loves; Robby and Beth are now sixteen and seventeen years old and they are still together. Robby adores Beth. He worships the ground she walks on and though she tried so hard to act like she didn't like him in the beginning, she eventually came around and didn't mind everyone knowing how much she loves him. They've been together since before I found them kissing in the barn that day so many years ago.

Beth would do anything for Robby, and often has, leading her to get into a lot of trouble, but he was right there to bail her out every time. When they were fourteen and fifteen, he talked her into climbing the town's water tower to spray paint their initials on it. I couldn't tell you why this girl would listen to him, and crawl up that tower, but she did. Their initials are still there in a big pink heart, but they both spent the night in jail. My parents and Darry's parents had refused to come get them, saying they needed to learn a lesson.

They must have learned that lesson too, because their stunts after that were much tamer, like tipping cows and toilet papering people's yards in the middle of the night. Whatever they do though, it's always together.

Beth even voluntarily took summer courses last summer so she could be in the same Senior class as Robby. She wanted to graduate the same time he did, so they wouldn't have to wait another year to start their lives together. Beth comes around to help out in the gift shop and Robby is Daddy's right-hand man. They're both learning the businesses so they can graduate and come right into them with us.

Mom and Elaine are already planning their wedding.

CHAPTER THIRTY-SEVEN

I'm sitting on the front porch, rocking and sipping my fresh squeezed lemonade. The air is cool and brisk on my skin; I love when Fall starts to sweep in. The weather is good for a few more weeks before the chill sets in. We're currently in the middle of nice weather, and as fleeting as it may be, I'll take it.

Noah's kicking me like crazy, while I watch Dally and Nate run around the pumpkin patch, as usual. Kevin's in the house washing his hands; he's just finished loading a truck full of pumpkins onto a pickup for the church. We'll be painting them with the kids in children's church this Wednesday night.

We have one week left for the trail to pull in as many visitors as possible before we have to begin closing it down due to the weather. Last year we did pretty well to keep it open a few weeks longer than we'll be able to this year. It's cooler this month than it usually is.

"Hey babe, what ya doin out here? Enjoying the last of the good weather?" Kevin asks as he sits in the rocking chair next to mine. "Look at those two, running around those pumpkins, not a care in the world, right?"

I nod in agreement and take a sip of my drink. "They love each other. It warms my heart to watch them together." I tell him, smiling at our daughter.

"Makes me think of you and Darry, a little bit. That's just how the two of you always were." Kevin says, a hint of sadness in his voice.

"Yeah. Me too." Is all I can say back to him.

He leans over and puts his hand on my belly, then he puts his mouth to it and says, "How are you doing in there, little boy? Aren't you ready to come out yet? We sure are ready to meet you, and today is a good day for being born." He sits up and kisses me, moving the hair out of my face and tucking it behind my ear. "You sure do look beautiful today, my love. Pregnancy looks really good on you. I think I'm gonna have to keep you this way." He says, winking at me, a suggestive grin coming up at the sides of his mouth.

"Ugh! I think I'm gonna need to take some time to recover after this one, thank you", I remind him.

My pregnancy with Dally was a breeze, this one not so much. I've had a difficult time, which is why I haven't been able to get out in the fields with the guys this year.

"I'm tired and I would like to not be fat for a while." I tell him, looking down at my swollen ankles.

This little boy is strong, and he has wreaked havoc on my tiny, delicate body. The doctor's have told me to take it easy, to stay off of my feet as much as possible. No hard work, no lifting of any kind; I can't even keep up my exercise routine, which is why I have gained a little more weight this time around.

Kevin gets up, standing in front of me. He reaches down for my hands and pulls me to my feet.

He kisses me and then begins to slow dance with me on the front porch. "You, my dear, are not fat. You are gorgeous and sexy, and you are carrying our child." He dips me as far as he can without hurting me and bends down to let his lips brush lightly against my neck, knowing it drives me crazy when he does it. I wrap my arms around his neck and let him guide me along the floor, as he sings softly to me in a whispered voice.

"This is why we're going to have ten kids, Kevin!" I tell him, feeling the blood begin to warm in my veins. He just grins at me, and spins me again, bringing me back into his arms when I come back around to face him.

"I don't mind ten kids." He says, his eyes darkening and his face taking on a look of sheer desire.

My pulse quickens and I can feel my heart beating fast against my chest. I love and hate how he can say something to me and look at me in such a way that I no longer have control over myself, it's all him; I am his to do with what he will. My heart bursts every time he looks at me like this; his eyes darken and all he sees is me, and all he wants... is me. It's overwhelming.

He scoops me up in his arms and carries me to the door, kicking open the screen, we move into the house, seamlessly.

"What about the kids?" I ask him, feeling a little panicky about leaving them outside.

"Your dad and Matt are out there, Alley. I think they'll be fine.'

We go into the bedroom and he lies me on the bed, lifting himself over me, he bends down to kiss me, moving from my lips to my neck and down my body.

He's exploring now and when he's like this, it's difficult for me to think of anything else. The ache he always seems to have for me in his eyes, burns straight through me; his stare stirring things inside of me and I'm all his.

He's so sweet and attentive, moving very slowly, making sure to focus on me as much as possible. He watches me with such intensity, such love; so full of longing, it makes my heart flutter and my blood run warm. After four years, he hasn't lost his intense desire for me, he never bores of me or loses interest. It's like he's with me for the first time, every time.

He lays back on his pillows, holding my hand to his chest, it rises and falls as he tries to catch his breath. I can feel his heart pounding underneath my hand. "I love you, Alley" he breathes, bringing my hand to his lips. I roll over and lay my head on his chest, "I love you too, Kevin... so much more than I'll ever be able to tell you." He kisses the top of my head and we both lay there for a few minutes just holding each other.

The house is quiet, and for the moment, there are no machines roaring outside of our bedroom window. We can hear Dally and Nate playing, squealing and laughing as they chase each other around the yard just beyond our bedroom. We lie in bed, holding one another, listening to the happy sounds of children enjoying a carefree life, and Kevin says to me, "For all of their happiness, we must be doing something right, ya know?"

I smile at his sweet, loving fatherly observation and tell him, "Absolutely. Those two are some of the happiest children I think I've ever known in my life. They know they are loved."

He sits up and leans over my belly, putting his hands on either side, he kisses me and looks up at me, whispering, "and so will he."

We collect ourselves and head outside to check on the kids and to watch the sunset before making dinner.

I sit on my rocking chair and look over at Dally and Nate who are now sitting in the dirt in the middle of the field between our houses, picking petals off of flowers.

Over by the barn I see Robby leaning over the corral, kissing Beth. They laugh together as she lets her head fall back, her hair trailing down her back. I watch them for a few minutes, noticing how Robby can't keep his hands off of her; even if he's simply brushing his hand down her arm, or moving a stray strand of hair from her face, he's affectionate toward her, always attentive.

I know instantly that he gets that from our daddy. Daddy is the same way with Mom, even now, after being married for as long as they have been, he still touches her constantly. It's sweet, and I silently pray that Kevin is always like that with me; even when we're older and we have ten kids!

Kevin looks over at me and follows my stare to see the couple fawning all over each other down by the horses. He smiles and squeezes my hand, "Aren't they adorable?" He says, somewhat teasing, but I can hear the sentiment in his tone. He loves them, and I know he's glad they have each other too.

"Yeah, they are." I reply, squeezing his hand back and then reaching up to kiss him.

Epilogue

The room is dark when I wake up, sweating, with severe cramping and pain in my lower back. I lay in bed for a few minutes, counting my contractions, trying to focus on the soft melodic breathing coming from beside me to take my mind off of the pain. We've had this happen more than once, and it turned out to be Braxton Hicks, so waking Kevin up at this point, is last resort.

When the back pain intensifies and the contractions are coming closer and closer together, consistently, I know it's time to wake him and start preparing to leave for the hospital.

The excitement is immediate, beginning with Kevin and spreading with every phone call he makes. Pretty soon our little house is full of sleepy, anxious people, all ready to meet Noah.

"Dad, will you please grab the bag by the door while I go get Dally, please?" Kev asks, pointing toward the little duffle bag by the front door.

"Sure thing, son." He says, nodding and walking away.

Kev races down the hall to Dally's room and wakes her up, telling her it's time to meet baby Noah. She sits up, dazed from being pulled out of her sleep. Rubbing her eyes, she asks, "Is Nate going too?"

"No, baby, he's sleeping, his mommy's mom is with him, but he will be there tomorrow. Promise." Kevin tells her, leaning down to kiss her nose.

She gets up and pulls her robe on over her nightgown and slips her tiny feet into her little lamb bedroom slippers. She's grown quite a bit and though her room has changed some over the past few years, she still holds tightly to her love of lambs.

We leave for the hospital, having quite the impressive caravan following behind us. We ride through town, Kev is going as fast as possible while still trying to maintain a cautious speed, knowing I will flip out if he races through town. But I can tell he's nervous and trying very hard to keep from going as fast as his heart is beating.

I'm trying to focus on my breathing, wanting to do what we learned in Lamaze class, but it's impossible. I know I'm breathing too fast, and it's not really helping how it should, but the pain is intense, and I can't focus how I need to be.

"Mommy, are you ok?" Dally asks from the backseat, concern growing in her little voice as the contractions cause me to groan and shift a lot.

"I'm... fine... baby. Your brother is just very ready to come out and meet everyone." I tell her, trying to reassure her that everything will be ok.

Kevin puts his hand on my knee, turning to look at me, checking on me and maybe checking to make sure there isn't a baby making his way into the car. I can see the tension all over his rigid body, and the anxiety in his stunning green eyes. "I'm ok, Kevin, really. Just focus on the road please", I tell him, reaching up to turn his face forward. He nods and puts his hand back on the wheel.

When we pull up to the door, Kevin comes around and opens the door, helping me out he walks me over to the wheelchairs and sits me down, going back for Dally. My daddy hops into the driver seat of Kevin's truck and parks it for us, so we can get right into the emergency room. I called my midwife before we left the house, so she'd know to be here. I look around, searching faces, looking for her, but she's not there.

Kevin noticing my apprehension, turns away from the nurse's desk and kneels down in front of me, placing both hands on my knees. "She's probably already upstairs, babe, it'll be ok."

I nod, continuing my Lamaze breathing. Dally is with my mom as we all wait for the nurse to find someone to escort us to the labor and delivery floor. Suddenly there's a puddle underneath me and my gown is soaked.

"Um... Kevin?" I say, trying to discreetly bring his attention to my situation.

He looks over and seeing the puddle, his eyes widen with fear and he tells the nurse, "Look, we know where to go, her water's just broke, I'm taking her up now, send security after us if you need to, but I'm not waiting for an escort to get here."

He grabs the wheelchair and turns me around to face the

elevators. With everyone following closely behind us, we head upstairs, having to take two elevators to get us all there.

As we come to Labor and Delivery, I see my midwife leaning over the nurse's desk, propped up on her elbows, talking to one of the male nurse's, flirting. I'm about to bring forth life from my body and she's here on my time, trying to find someone to take home. I'm not sure that I'm really ok with this scenario at this moment.

When we get closer to her, she turns and seeing me, her eyes get very big, very quick, and I know in that instance that I must look rough.

"Yeah, ok, let's get ya'll to a room. I don't think we should drag feet by the looks of you, young lady." She tells me, coming around to grab my chair to wheel me into the room directly across from the nurse's station.

My labor is quick and within the hour, we have a healthy, happy baby boy with amazing green eyes and a head full of wavy brown hair.

The nurse hands him to me, and Kevin leans in, kissing his forehead, he whispers, "Welcome to the world, little boy. You are already so dearly loved."

I am one happy momma with one thrilled, proud daddy and a room full of excited grandparents, aunts and uncles, and one completely in love big sister.

I love my family, and I'm so thankful to God for each

and every one of them. I couldn't imagine my life any other way.

ABOUT THE AUTHOR

Tina Arnold is the author of the Sweet Lantern series. At 38 years old, she currently resides in Georgia, with her husband, Johnnie, and her four children, Clara, Marian, Kathryn, and Aiden. Currently she is working on her bachelor's degree in Early Childhood Development, writing, and staying active within her church. She attends church regularly along with weekend prayer groups as well as a women's bible study.